ACE HIGH

A NOVELLA, A SHORT STORY

AND A PEEK

BY

KEN BYERS

Copyright 2016
Published by Lloyd Court Press
Portland, OR
ISBN 978-1-943640-00-3

ACE HIGH – Two Stories each with its own look at death and life from author Ken Byers –

In *Final Notice,* a widow's late husband losses their retirement money in a scam that bilks thousands of retirees out of their peace of mind. After her husband dies, Marcella Packer is left alone to figure her life out. She manages until the day the bank's Final Notice darkens her mail box. She is to be evicted and left to a life on the streets. She organizes what little is left and prepares to end her ordeal. On her final walk around town, on her way to disappear into the ocean forever, fate steps in and delivers a whole new plan.

In the longer story, a rugged and battle-scarred ex-GI, full name Daniel Thomas Spader, or Dan T to his friends, and Ace to those who know the story of his intimate tattoo, roams the streets of Island City looking for a killer. In *Ace,* the characters Dan T meets on his search have all had miraculous escapes from death, many in the recently concluded World War II. Versions of the story become so common and echo his own, that Dan T sees a new mystery with far greater implications. Add the disturbing sense of having done it all before, and Dan T's search becomes an existential journey in search of transcendence while answers to traditional questions fade into the impenetrable and ever-present mist of Island City.

At the end of Ace please find the first chapter of Ken Byers's book *Laughland* as a thank you for reading.

FINAL NOTICE

Ken Byers

A Not So Short Story

To Begin with . . .

The discovery of a neatly stacked pile of clothes on the sand just south of the Eleventh Street beach access was the first thing that told Sheriff Carl Fredericks he had a problem. The spot was well known to the locals as a dangerous place to play because of the under-tow.

Bad place to play, he thought, but a good place for suicide.

He had been at lunch when the call came. He asked if they found any identification.

"Yeah, Sheriff," said deputy Gordon Sails. "An envelope in the pocket addressed to Marcella Packer. Has a big "Final Notice" stamp on it from some bank."

"Goddamn-it!" he said, too loudly and then had to look a sheepish apology around the crowded restaurant. "I'll be there in a couple of minutes."

When he arrived he and his deputy stood looking at the clothes. He fumbled through them and found a coat with a hat, along with shoes and old lady knee-highs all neatly arranged on the sand just above the high tide mark. He looked at the envelope.

"She was losing her house to the bank," Fredericks said. "I asked her if she'd be okay. She said she had a plan."

They both kicked the sand before the deputy said, "I guess this was it."

The sheriff shook his head. "Pick it up and bag it. I'll go look at her house."

Before he reached his car he got two calls. The first was a fatal car wreck near the casino and the second came less than a minute later about a robbery at a bar at the south end. He didn't get to Marcella Packer's house that day. Then he forgot about it. By the time he did get there two days had passed and he did no more than a cursory inspection to verify the house was empty. He knocked at the neighbor's place. Old Crystal Thorgard told him she hadn't seen a light for a few days. She was about to call because she was worried. Marcella didn't go anywhere, she said. She had no money. Poor thing.

ACE HIGH by Ken Byers

Marcella

I

On the first day of February's annual False Spring – clear sunny days that promised daffodils but always disappointed – Marcella stared at the words Final Notice on the envelope that had just dropped into her mail box. The higher-on-the-right angle insured that the capital letters of the stamp's red ink didn't overlay the addressee. Her. Marcella Packer. On Seacliff Street in Lincoln City, Oregon. The upper left simply said Pacific Coast Mortgage and Trust, Salem, Oregon.

After the two years of speculation as to how she would feel when this dreaded letter finally darkened her table top, she realized she felt nothing. Feeling nothing surprised her. She'd imagined every emotion she'd ever felt. Even exotic combinations, such as a melding of grief and elation, or fury and steel-eyed determination. The emptiness of the moment left her disoriented.

After Ralph left her and it was her job to get the mail, she carefully planned a daily ritual in anticipation of the

ACE HIGH by Ken Byers

arrival of the Final Notice. She only retrieved the mail on Tuesdays, Thursdays, and Saturdays. When Saturday delivery ended she adjusted to Tuesdays and Fridays. On the appropriate days she opened the hip-high nine-by-twelve-inch wooden door of the mail drop to the right of the front door. Most of her post consisted of catalogues and offers from companies that made goods she'd purchased in a past life. These companies kept sending their slick and colorful advertisements not realizing she could no longer afford them. It was a rarity to find any mail with her address handwritten – really handwritten, not machine-printed with that fake look – and even more rarely did she receive a personal letter from someone she actually knew. She always sorted the mail into stacks from left to right. First came recyclables, then trash, and to the right the few that required some action on her part. This last stack comprised mainly bills and envelopes that, in one way or another, said Final Notice. One by one each of these painful, life-rending notices shrank her existence as she paid to keep the heat or the lights on, or to hold on to the other pitifully few necessities she required to keep body and breath wedded.

"Shit," she said to the envelope from Pacific Coast Mortgage and Trust bearing the dreaded ultimate Final Notice. She said the word aloud and looked out the window as if checking to see if anyone might have heard. Crystal Thorgard walked, cane in hand, toward the sidewalk. No way had Crystal heard. She didn't hear when you stood in front of her and spoke loudly.

"Crystal would never say shit," Marcella said, still out loud as if testing Crystal's hearing, as she rapped the still unopened envelope on the table. "But then a year ago, maybe two years ago, I didn't say it either. Wouldn't dream of it." She dropped the envelope to the right of the other items.

She sighed and closed her eyes as she waited for what she knew would follow. On cue she heard the voice that now only spoke in her head say, "Lot of water under the bridge, old girl." The voice, shaped by time into a two-edged blade, carved at her heart each day. It mocked her, drove her to the use of words like the one she'd just uttered, but it was also her only company. It was Ralph's voice, his mocking – no – his *sarcastic* tone that he used to hurt her. The older they got the better she became at fighting with him and protecting herself. The last thing he'd ever said to her was in that tone. It was the way she remembered him.

She sighed and put him out of her mind. Into the emotional void pushed the envelope. It flooded her with a rush of pain as it merged with Ralph. He'd left her with no warning. One day he was there; the next day gone. When it came to thoughts of Ralph, if not for pain, she would have no feelings at all. She turned her head to the left – toward the mirror atop the buffet that lined that side of the dining room – and smiled. She looked closer to be sure she smiled – that she hadn't just imagined she'd smiled meaning her face no longer remained capable of forming a smile. She saw the smile and knew that in some ways she still lived. She saw the smile in the mirror's reflection to the right of the urn that held Ralph. The position meant she remained to his left and slightly behind. On different planes, yes, but that was always the case in one way or the other. The dutiful wife always a step behind on the subservient side. She had decided years ago that she would not be buried to his left. Compliant in life was enough. Not all women felt this way. A committee member she served with on Loaves and Fishes told her of a woman who had her mother disinterred because the funeral parlor had buried the woman on the wrong side of her husband which meant they could not be together in heaven. Marcella listened politely and clicked her tongue in apparent sympathy but thought the whole thing ridiculous. Why would a woman want to spend eternity with her husband?

That brought her back to the Final Notice. With the envelope still flat on the table, her fingers traced the faded red letters on the cheap bond envelope. The stamp's ink pad used by Pacific Coast Mortgage and Trust must have needed inking. Perhaps they sent out piles of such letters to others like her all needing that red stamp. She felt slighted. This letter would do more to damage her survival chances than any of the previous demands from other creditors. Perhaps more than all the others combined. The bank could have used a better quality envelope for something of this importance. In a way it announced a death; it deserved a wrapper commensurate with the message.

Because she had known this day would come, she had made inquiries as to how long she might have before the sheriff would lock her out. Her many volunteer activities included handing out coffee and cookies to the faithful on Sundays after church. One of the regulars was the sheriff, the very one who would one day have to evict her. When it was clear her curiosity was no longer idle, she acted. The memory of the conversation months ago remained clear.

As she took Sheriff Carl Fredericks aside she told him her plight.

"Someday you will come to my house to put me out on the street." He tensed and she lightly took his arm. "Not your fault. The reason I am telling you this is so I can plan. I need to find out how long I will have from the day I receive the final notice."

"I am sorry to hear this, Mrs. Packer," Sheriff Fredericks said. "We have a lot of them these days. Probably doesn't make you feel any better, but it does slow things down."

"Slows down how much?"

"Evictions – once we have the paper-work, which takes a few weeks – require organization. It's hard on everyone in a town like this where people know their neighbors." He sipped his coffee and took a bite off one of the cookies on his little paper plate. "All in all, nothing less than thirty days and usually sixty to ninety days. For you it will be at least ninety. We have a little leeway."

She smiled and patted his arm in thanks.

"But, Mrs. Packer, we will be coming. It's the law."

"Oh, Sheriff, I'm not asking for anything special. I just wonder. Do you call for an appointment or just show up with a big lock?"

He smiled and shook his head. "Nothing quite that dramatic. We will try to work it out with you to make it as painless as possible."

"Thank you. Will the man from the bank be there?"

"No. Just their paperwork."

"They don't even send a person to take away the most important thing in my world?"

Sheriff Fredericks shrugged.

"Doesn't seem right," she said. "Another cookie, Sheriff?"

"What will you do? There are services. They're stretched, but they're still there. I don't want to worry about you."

She smiled up at him and patted his arm again.

"No worry needed," she said. "When the day comes I'm sure I'll know what to do."

Bobby

I

Robert J. "Bobby" Cain whistled while he shaved. To his right on the stainless steel shelf at elbow height on the twelve-foot mirror that lined the wall and reached to the ceiling of the walk-through bathroom, and above the "his and her" sinks stood his Samsung tablet. The high definition screen displayed a webcast of the morning's financial news. He smiled as all the stock indicators showed that 401K's and other geezer accounts were swimming along nicely across the board swelling funds that Bobby and his phone-mates would soon transfer to their own *very early* retirement accounts stashed in faraway places.

His smile dimmed as Grayson Fitzpatrick's face filled the screen. The only time the somber network anchor managed screen time was with bad news. The crawler beneath his face stopped carrying stock prices on a blue background. It now screamed BREAKING NEWS in white on red. Bobby turned up the volume.

"Just minutes ago in Washington D.C.," Fitzpatrick droned in his funereal tone with its deliberate pacing that left the listener hanging and waiting for the next nail to be driven into their heart, "the Justice Department announced a long list of indictments against the so-called 'Fish in a Barrel' section of reeling energy giant ENCO Solutions. The indictments accuse specific managers, traders and salespeople with systematically draining hundreds of thousands of senior savings accounts using illegally obtained insider information from a sister division."

Bobby Cain dropped his razor. Had he been shaving his throat, his neck would now be bleeding. He reached to pick the razor up but his hands trembled so much he fumbled it around the sink.

The name 'Fish in a Barrel', Fitzpatrick went on to say, came from a wiretap recording of two traders laughing about how easy it was to fleece seniors of their savings. One said it was like shooting fish in a barrel. It hit the Internet and set a record for reaching a million hits faster than any post in history. The story made the network news that night. By the next morning, the parent oil company – never mind that other energy sources and programs were a major part of the company's income –

went from perceived evil to no-doubt-about-it-evil bottom suckers.

The border of the screen on Bobby's tablet pulsed in red alerting him to an incoming call. He looked at the caller ID and answered. The caller, Andrew Misnick, sat in the cubicle next to Bobby. "Bobster! You watching Fitzpatrick? Jesus! Is that us? We goin' to jail?"

"I don't know," Bobby said.

"Can't be us!" Misnick yelled into the phone. "Shit, we aren't even middle management. We're pissant management!"

"Hey, man, we laughed at Fish in a Barrel, too."

"It wasn't us on that tap!" Misnick said, voice ratcheting toward panic.

"Yeah, but we both told Doug and Mitchell they were dumb shits for getting recorded. But Andy, it could have been us."

"I know, I know! Christ. I was just trying to get rich!"

Bobby wiped at the foggy glass of the mirror guaranteed never to cloud. He realized the futility of his action and wondered what he was really trying to see.

"What are you going to do, Bobster?" The panic had cooled to a whine in Misnick's voice.

Bobby continued staring at his reflection before answering. "I'm going to work. I'm going to wear my best suit, walk into the office with my head held high like I've done nothing wrong, which, in my opinion, I haven't. I presented investment opportunities to people who had liquidity. Maybe we sold harder than we should have, but there's no real fraud. Their money isn't lost. They have stocks that still have a value."

Misnick hesitated and then said in a voice devoid of hope, "You know we over-sold that shit. You know it, I know it, and so do the authorities. What happens when that stock tanks?" He hung up.

Bobby raised his chin and patted underneath his tanned and still firm skin with the top of his hand. It was something he'd seen in a movie. He saw it as a self-congratulatory motion; the kind of thing a successful man still in his prime does before he puts on his best suit and knots his silk tie.

After he kissed his beautiful wife and two kids, and as he drove his BMW 750i toward the office, he was tempted to leave the radio off but his need to know overrode his common sense. By the time he reached the parking garage ENCO Solutions' stock had dropped forty-seven percent in the last hour and was still falling at the rate of an express elevator. The stocks his group had been touting were the first to crash. By the time he opened the outer door of the twenty-second floor office everyone there looked gut-shot.

Katrina, the woman who ran the office with a firm but smooth hand, said, "Corporate called. They said to expect the marshals within the hour."

After the hurricane of the same name there were jokes about her name, but Bobby doubted anyone laughed today even with the impact of her words.

He nodded, and asked, "Bud in yet?" Bud Connaught managed the local unit.

Katrina shook her head. "His cellphone's turned off and no one answers his home phone. I called Mimsy's cell and she said he got a call about two in the morning. He said nothing to her. Just packed a bag and left. When she heard the news this morning she told me she didn't think he'd be back."

Bobby stared at her. "He just left her?"

"Mimsy called him a chicken-shit bastard. She said he would have left for less. He cleaned out their savings and retirement funds late yesterday but she didn't check until today. She doesn't know where the money went."

Bobby caught the irony of the vanished savings as he felt his shoulders slump. The top guys learned yesterday and bugged out with their bucks in hand and their mouths shut. Bobby knew with all his heart they were gone not to be heard from again from any country with extradition to the United States.

"Somebody has to stand in the courtroom," he said. He looked around the office at the people who listened to them. Everyone stared at him.

The door behind him burst open. He turned to see a riot of television reporters and camera people with blindingly bright lights burst in. Several shouted at him and Katrina demanding to know who was in charge. He shrugged. She pointed at him. Camera lights swung toward him pinning him to the floor the way a bug would be in biology. Microphones appeared in his face.

"How many old people did you fleece?" was the question he heard above the cacophony. He reeled. Later, when he saw the clip, he saw he'd done more than reel. His skin faded beyond a sickly white to a pale green that might explode over the reporters. Some hurriedly pulled back. Others risked all and waited for the answer Bobby failed to provide. Days later his attorney praised him for keeping his mouth shut, but Bobby knew the truth. He froze. Not a word to be found and no breath to utter one even if he had. He escaped into the men's room and into a stall where he made noises that discouraged anyone from following him. A half hour later he came out. The lobby of the office stood empty. The ship had sunk and the rats were long gone. He walked out the door knowing he would never return.

He ignored the elevators and used the stairs. In the time it took to walk down twenty-two flights he had no long range plan. What he did know was that Robert J. Cain had a family. He was not like that chicken-shit bastard Bud Connaught, his former boss, who could disappear into the deep Pacific where a tropical island would serve as a jail of its own kind. Bobby's views on right and wrong maybe were flexible and he wanted to be as rich as his youthful dreams had promised him he would become, but he would not abandon his family. He would revisit that idea several times in the upcoming months.

His first stop on the street was the haberdashery down the block, where he bought a hat with a wide brim. He pulled it down before returning to the parking garage where he'd left his car. He placed his briefcase in the trunk and walked up the ramp to the street.

He traveled one block to his personal bank with the secret safe deposit box. He went in, ignored the stares of people in the bank who knew him for his large deposits and numerous trips to his box in the safe, and emptied the box into a case stored there for this purpose. On the top of the cash, bearer bonds, and stock certificates, he laid out the new identity bought and richly paid for with this day in mind but no real conviction that it would ever come. He drove to a small boutique bank located in a new, discreet high-rise catering to financial businesses. The bank specialized in expediting foreign deposits. Bobby opened an account with his alternate identity and took care of his recent riches so that they would remain his. Or at least as much his as the times would allow. Lots of question marks there.

He needed more help.

Forty minutes later he found a church with its doors open. He walked in and prayed that he would not go to jail. It was the first time he'd been in a church since his wedding. He went to a second church several hours later and prayed his recently squirreled away offshore money would not be taken by some misguided legal system. He liked the second church better than the first. It was Episcopalian and had a kneeling bench. Being on his knees fit his level of desperation. A birch rod would have been good too. He would lash his back with strokes that would shred his suit coat and silk shirt. God had to know he was serious about this repentance business. He had a family, for Christ's sake!

Marcella

II

The two women who would call Marcella their friend and another five who would, after consideration, describe their relationship with her as "cordial," all thought of her as level headed, and above any act of violence. Much later, when authorities asked them those very questions they all emphatically said that was not her at all. The women were also asked if any of them had ever seen Marcella walking the streets and talking to herself. They were all shocked and even more emphatic in their denials. During questioning, one woman revised her answer and did mention she recalled seeing Marcella talking to herself one day not long before the incident, and thought it odd. She said it was not like Marcella to talk to someone who wasn't there. Even with that last comment in mind, the one making the revision said Marcella Packer was dependable. She was grounded. She was a member of committees both at her church and in the community. She did what she was asked to do and never argued. No one could remember her ever uttering the dreaded, "or we could do it this way" to confuse and muck things up. This last quality endeared her to many a committee chair.

One thing noted by a solitary voice out of the many women interviewed in the aftermath said that Marcella was the best listener in the whole parish. She always listened to everyone's problems, even the most insignificant drivel, and made polite and sometimes insightful comments. The odd thing was that she never shared any of her own, and obviously she must have had them. They all knew her husband had mishandled their retirement money and lost it all, but you would never know it from sharing a committee job with Marcella. The woman closed her interview by saying that if this is what happened when you kept your problems corked up then she was going to be more forthcoming. She wouldn't care what anyone thought.

What eventually followed would prove to be perplexing to all who knew her and those who didn't.

Marcella awoke the morning after the arrival of the Final Notice exhausted of body, but peaceful of mind. It was the first day of what life she had left. Decisions had been reached in the panoply of her dreams which stretched from a childhood she had only the vaguest memory of to death – a death she saw as not too distant. She replayed them as she fixed her coffee and used a scoop more from the Yuban tin than usual. No more worries about caffeine, she thought. Or running out before she could afford more.

"No more worries at all," she said aloud and smiled ruefully as she sipped the first cup being sure to appreciate the extra taste. She'd made three cups, which was one more cup than usual. She would savor them all while she wrote in her dream diary.

The dream diary was new since Ralph had left and had become part of her regular routine. It's how she started the day. She had begun the practice less than a week after Ralph's ashes appeared on her buffet centered so that when she sat at the table and stacked the mail, she could glance to her left and see her reflection side by side with him. Other times she adjusted the chair so the position she'd spent most of her life in with him – behind him and almost out of sight – was what she saw.

Her dreams became richer in content and texture following his death so it seemed fitting to tell him, or his urn, all about what she'd experienced and thought in her sleep. The urn proved to be an unsatisfying audience. The next day she moved the dream diary she kept beside her bed to the dining room and laid it next to the urn. The following morning, she started writing in it while she had her coffee.

In the beginning of Life After Ralph, the very first thing she'd said to the urn had nothing to do with her dreams. She'd said, "Now *I* get the last word." It was a sweet notion that pleased her deeply but it didn't last; he started arguing with her in her dreams that very night. The dream diary showed just how much he argued with her and how often she still did what he told her to do. The process of writing these defeats down had already started a new resolve within her. Soon she would be strong enough to ignore him. Laughing at him would be the next step.

Last night's dreams, the first night after the Final Notice arrived, were a powerful example of the Battle for the Last Word. Not quite asleep as she lay in her bed with the comforter pulled up, she decided it was time to call it quits. Soon the bank would take her house and she would have no place to live. She had no close family (Ralph's Great Failing in that he failed to fertilize any of her eagerly awaiting eggs). No friends she would ever dream of imposing on, either. She might find a charity if she got on a list right away to help her find affordable housing, but with so many seniors suffering the same fate the demand may have exceeded the hearts of the community. Even if she found something it was no way to live out your final years, and even if she did have a few more good years, what would she do with them? Simply put, she would rather die.

"Goddamn-it, woman!" Ralph thundered in her dream. She felt the bed shake. Maybe her body jerked at the psychic battering and that was why the bed moved. Maybe it was because his spirit gripped the frame and lifted it. If so, he had more strength in death than she had in life.

"You have lots of reasons to live!' Ralph yelled into her dream. He listed off several reasons she should live that he would like – such as joining the woman's club at the golf course, or maybe taking a cruise to Mexico – but nothing she had any interest in. Plus, she had no money for travel and golf lessons. She couldn't even afford to pay for her pottery supplies or to fire her kiln unless she paid the gas bill. His blatant disregard for fiscal reality continued to literally haunt her from the grave.

He thundered and blustered in the dream, and the bed continued to shake. Sitting at the table she was now sure the bed actually did shake. No way was it her imagination. It occurred to her that the shaking bed may have been her fault, as she gave birth to ideas heretofore unthinkable.

Ralph had said, "Take a look around your world. It's not that bad."

She did look around her world using his telescope in the glass-encased turret at the top of the house. They'd added the bubble to the roof before they moved in so they could see both the ocean and the lake. Seacliff Street was neither on the sea nor on a cliff. It sat astride the ridge that formed the high ground between the Pacific Ocean to the west and Devil's Lake to the east.

The crest was also the line between ocean fog and lake sunshine. The turret pushed the view above the fog when their neighbors on the ridge were blinded by the moist goo formed by local weather conditions known to all as the Gray Gloom. Using the telescope, no more than feet above the depressing fog, had kept her spirits high through many a worry-wracked day. Now that the big new house on the lake was finished she missed one of her favorite sights. No more did cranes lift joists and shingles. No more did workers swarm over the house nailing and painting. It was a wonder watching the beautiful house take shape. She'd made the sight her own to the point of feeling proprietarily about it. The five gables faced directly at her and she'd wondered how many people it would take to fill a house like that. These thoughts had helped for months. Now people had moved in. They'd taken the house from her.

She set her coffee cup down, cleared her throat, and said, "Ralph, listen close. This will be the last time you hear me speak these words. Ready? Here they come." She cleared her throat. "I quit. Without you yelling at me all night, I might have dithered without the resolve to make the decision." She stiffened her back and rapped the table top with her knuckles. "Now I have decided."

She thought she sensed a rumbling deep within her chest but wrote it off to the burst of caffeine hitting her system no doubt jangling her nerves and tweaking her fancy that seemed to have been given a jolt in the night.

She picked up her napkin, dabbed at the corner of her mouth, and then with enthusiasm, she systematically wiped her hands before carefully setting the cloth next to her coffee cup.

With no future to plan for, her thoughts focused on the past. She decided to give herself a report card like you receive when you finish a class. Life, they said, was a learning process and her life was about over. In grade school, grades were letter grades: C as in commendable, S as in satisfactory, and N as in needs improvement.

She started with citizenship. That one was easy. She got a C. She had been faithful to Ralph even when he had not. She'd been hostess, chef, photographer, chauffeur, and even babysat out of town wives so Ralph could sell something to their husbands. She had never complained and always performed up to expectations, if he had any, but always to hers and hers were high. She had her pride.

She gave herself a C- in home ec. She'd never been a good cook. She could pull it together for Ralph and

ACE HIGH by Ken Byers

friends for special occasions after scanning cook-books and careful planning, but when it came to whipping something up from odds and ends in the cupboards or fridge she was a flop. She had no heart or soul for food. She thought about it some more, dwelling on the disasters, but realistically she'd done a good job when the chips were down, and for that she deserved at least the C-. As for the rest of housekeeping, she was a solid if not spectacular housewife. Tidy was important, but the white glove test was never practiced in her home.

The card had its share of N's. This first came in spontaneity. She was terrible at knowing what to do when Ralph or anyone else said What do you want to do? She never had a suggestion beyond something they had done recently. She had gone so far as to read dining guides and the entertainment section in the newspaper so she would have some ideas if asked. On the rare occasion when she was asked her mind went blank. Had there been a grade below N she would have given it to herself.

Reading and spelling got C's. She loved to read. She was also a very good speller, so good in fact that Ralph had her check his reports and proposals.

She gave herself an N in math. She was not good with money. So bad she'd left it up to Ralph and therein lay the reason for the predicament in which she now found herself. It was also the reason he found himself in an urn on the buffet and not in a bed down the hall snoring his nights away. He couldn't deal with the reality of losing their retirement income.

She gave herself one C+. In artistic endeavor. She potted. In fact, she'd made the urn in which Ralph's ashes now reposed. For a woman with woefully slight imagination and limited colors, her pottery was beautiful. In reality it all looked very similar and the first examples were derivative of a potter whose works she had always admired, but her execution was excellent. The decisions that went into the design and creation for Ralph's final resting place occupied her creative fancy for many an hour while he waited in a sturdy, unmarked cardboard box. The range of designs she considered reflected all the complex feelings she'd had for him including leaving him, in the box precariously close to the edge of the buffet with the flap undone. If it spilled, she'd have to clean it up just like while he was alive. The eventual winner was a subdued design that could mean anything. Also just like him.

That left just one class to grade. Call it retribution. N did not do her justice. For this one she gave herself an F as in failure. *Abject*, no excuses, failure! The thief, Robert J. Cain, happily wandered the planet spending their money. She could still hear Ralph repeating his litany of woe that began and ended with Cain's name. In her mind the F became a red F.

She refilled her coffee cup and walked into the dining room. She stared at herself in the mirror as she loomed over the urn. She cocked her head. Something was missing. She gave a quick decisive nod of her head and went into the room that had been Ralph's. She rarely entered the room she thought of as being just as dead as her departed. In the closet stood his golf clubs, spiked shoes and the other paraphernalia golfers swore they needed. On the bureau were bits and pieces of his other interests. Some items she had no idea as to their uses. She shook her head because the mysteries posed by the odd shaped this or that brought to mind one of the few times she let her petty side take over. She saw the items, wondered what they were and saw how he revered them, but then blocked questions out of her mind. Why should she show an interest? He'd never so much as applauded any of her raku, not even the pieces that had won ribbons at bazaars and fairs. She had her best pieces all over the house and Ralph never said a word. He simply couldn't be bothered.

He'd had one interest that had shown some practical application but it hadn't lasted. Soon after they moved here he'd outfitted his tool shop, as he called it, in a sturdy shed attached to the rear of the house. He stocked it with saws and hammers and nails and even some wood, but they just sat there while Ralph golfed or studied his stock tips or stared through his telescope. When his neglect of the space became chronic, she took over the shed. She was strong for her size. She stripped the shed down herself and put it to use as the mud-room for her potting. Her kiln, large enough to fire the substantial pieces she favored, sat outside the door all neatly hooked up to the natural gas so she could finish her creations. At its side was the chain hoist for lifting the heavier pieces. Because the room was damp, she kept her computer inside the house. She didn't know much about it, but she used it for designing her pieces and enlarging appealing designs she saw elsewhere. She didn't even do e-mail. To whom would she send such a thing? When money got tight she couldn't afford her pottery.

The reason for entering his dead room now sat in the top drawer of his desk, beneath the handgun he'd bought for their protection, and partially hidden by other papers, including the envelope with their passports. They were there as a reminder of another failed dream of retirement. She picked up the gun he had insisted she learn how to use and laid it aside to get the file folder. The papers were in their current order because after he left she'd rearranged them by date in search of something practical like life insurance, of which he had none.

Now her interest surged as this time she found what she wanted. It was an unlabeled manila file folder. On her way out she closed the door of the dead room, pawed through her craft basket in the kitchen for her scissors, and took everything to the dining room table. She put the file directly in front of her, then she picked up the Final Notice and flicked it with a finger before setting it squarely on top of the folder.

Bobby

II

Bobby Cain knew within fifteen minutes of his first invocation that he didn't want to be in church. It wasn't salvation he wanted. He wanted brownie points. He didn't want to go to jail, although by now that seemed less likely.

In the two and a half weeks since the Shit Hit the Fan the only indictments out were for top management types in Atlanta. The howls of protest from the masses had focused on the CEO, CFO, and a half dozen other initials and vice presidents after they appeared on the news. They did the usual disclaiming of any responsibility for the collapse and the disappearance of billions of dollars in pension funds and individual retirement packages, but no one believed them. The mass media called them scumbags and modern day carpetbaggers and other less flattering names. The only things these men had going for them– and they were all men – was that they hadn't joined the exodus to non-extradition tax havens. By now Bobby saw as remote the threat of prison time reaching all the way to the Pacific Coast. For sure the threat still existed, but that it would reach down and touch the life of someone as insignificant as a Glengarry Glen Ross-type salesman now seemed remote. Never mind the salesman had pocketed over six million dollars syphoned from the same pension plans and 401(k)'s the others had tapped. There had been a particularly unnerving moment when a political cartoon in the *New Yorker* portrayed a character that bore no physical resemblance to Bobby but in all other ways was Bobby to a T. The cartoon figure diverted a portion of the life savings of an old man sitting in a wheelchair. In the distance the cartoon showed a fat cat in a bathing suit largely hidden by the rolls of his stomach sipping a drink with an oversized bamboo umbrella. The man lay on a tropical island while the flow of money that got past Bobby went directly into a bulging carpetbag at the fat cat's side. It was enough to keep Bobby in church praying for deliverance despite the flood of hypocrisy that filled his communion cup. He had hoped church would make him feel better, but it didn't. All the talk about guilt hit too close to home although he continued to insist he didn't feel guilty.

Pacific Northwest papers in Seattle and Portland ran features on the Fish in the Barrel boys including pictures of each of the perpetrators including Bobby. In the weeks that followed he was recognized twice on the street, resulting in dangerous and embarrassing moments, but he survived. He didn't give up telling his friends and family that the story was blown way out of proportion and that he had cooperated with investigators while holding nothing back. This last part was superficially true thanks to Bobby's meticulous advanced planning. He had a separate set of books that revealed none of his squirreled away wealth. He had paid good money to be sure the books would stand any audit. In those weeks he spent escaping more retribution, he felt he had spent his money wisely.

As a child Bobby had received an allowance that was larger than what most of the kids in his class got. He knew in the way kids always know. They talk or they show off their purchases and word gets around. However, there were two or three kids Bobby was sure got substantially more than he did. He was envious. Not so much for what it would buy, because he had enough to get whatever he wanted, but he just wanted to have at least as much money as any of the kids he palled around with. This became a frustrating theme: close but no crown. His fraternity in college. After graduation with his MBA in the bars after work comparing bonuses. Dues at one club or another. Bobby was not top rung. He still wanted to be top rung, but now one thing had changed.

He didn't want anyone to know. He wasn't talking so if anyone knew, it meant he'd left a trail and that was not acceptable. A trail led to prison or making a break for it, which meant he would be leaving his life behind which was a mixed bag at best.

He loved his wife, who loved the things his money could buy. She had never voiced criticism of her husband's methods, meaning she didn't care enough to threaten the supply of money. She did not take the loss of his income stream gracefully, mostly because of the interruption of her cash flow rather than the threat of his incarceration. That latter point did bother her, because she would be pointed at as the wife of a "scumbag bloodsucker." Giselle Cain did not want to be pointed at for any reason other than her beauty and style. If she would be pressed, and she would be after the incident, as to whether she had ever loved Bobby she would answer with a tearful nod of her head but with eyes that said she was over him. It was a moment she would practice to perfection; a look that said more than words could ever say.

His world – apart from money – came down to his kids. Natty for Nathaniel, and Maddie for Madeline, were eight and six when the Shit Hit the Fan. They skated through the household tension, and the news was never big enough to reach their grade school. Not once did either come home and tell him the kids at school called their father a criminal. Or worse. He was grateful. The kids were reflections of their parents with Maddie being more like her father and Natty inheriting the good looks and slender form of his mother. Maddie's most noticeable takeaway from Bobby was her quick and occasionally devious mind, which made her older brother angry. If Bobby was in the room when his daughter effectively bamboozled his son she would look at him and give him a look that asked if that was the how he would have done it. Sometimes, for the really good ones, Bobby would nod and his daughter would run over and tell him she loved him.

With time to reflect while he worried about incarceration and exposure, Bobby wondered what he'd say if asked why he did it. Would he say to provide for his family? If he did, could he make it sound sincere? Was he sincere?

At the end of a long day of wondering, moments before sleep waylaid him thanks to a new medication, Bobby thought the reason he'd bilked so many out of so much was that he'd liked it. It wasn't much different from pinball. The lights flashed and the tote board numbers got larger. He won and others lost.

Marcella

III

She admired her finished work.

The grainy photo of Robert J. Cain she'd cut from the newspaper now looked grainier after being enlarged by her computer's software. She printed the result and then cut out the figure of the smiling man who waved as he walked out of a building. As the next step in her craft project, she glued the cutout to a cardboard back with a foldout foot so he would stand tall. Next to Ralph. On the buffet to Ralph's right.

She hadn't bothered to read the caption before cutting it off and discarding it. She didn't care about that. He was the man who had conned Ralph out of their lives and killed him. Not normally given to hyperbole, her sentiments carried even greater impact. She didn't know how Ralph knew this man Cain was *the* man. Maybe he wasn't, but Ralph always knew these kinds of things. He called it "ears in the city," or sometimes he called it "sniffing out the truth with your ear glued to the ground." How like him – the mixed metaphor.

On the day Robert J. Cain's picture entered their lives, Ralph yelled "Son of a bitch!" from his chair as he read the paper. Even in retirement Ralph read the paper in the same chair he always had and still drank three cups of coffee, actually two and a half because he never finished the third. He left the cup on the drain board for her to deal with which she did every day. It was the first thing she missed when he was gone.

"This is the guy, Marci!" he said, slapping the paper. "This is the goddamn thief that took our money."

Next came bluster that made Marcella feel low and depressed. When he was younger, Ralph never blustered. He did things. He had been a doer. To see him reduced to bluster made her sad for both of them.

"I would do anything to get back at that guy," Ralph often said in the mornings of the last few months of his life. Marcella knew he had become obsessed, and his inability to do anything about it ate at him until it eventually ate a hole in his heart.

"Do you know anything about him?" she finally asked one morning.

"Yeah! The asshole is rich with my money."

She didn't correct him, but her pension money had been in the pot Ralph had wagered as well.

"Besides that, what do you know?" she asked. "You can't do anything until you learn more about him."

"How the hell am I supposed to do that? Huh?"

"It does you no good to complain to me every morning. You're frustrated. This kind of behavior is doing you no good. It will kill you."

"Can't afford to live anyway,' he said, three days before his heart exploded.

For the longest time after Ralph entered the urn she didn't think about Robert J. Cain. The thief occasionally crossed her mind, but as soon as she sensed his shadow lurking she drove him away with a broom. Literally. She swept the kitchen floor, focusing intently until she thought of other things, things where she could make some kind of difference, even small ones, which usually meant a phone call to one committee or an increase in her volunteer activities. Sometimes both.

The ploy worked until the Final Notice.

Then the anger returned and with it came Robert J. Cain. Any thought of a "he'll get his in the afterworld" had long flown into her dark well of resentment, the well she could no longer deny. It materialized simultaneously with the conviction it was time to call it quits. That was logical. There was no revenge or retribution if she quit. She had never been much of a believer in pop anecdotes about nebulous subjects like letting go, or visualizing better places to ease her pain. Rather, she clung to it like a golden chain and let her hate for the damage to their lives at the hands of the thief whet the crystal sharp edge of her determination to end her life.

On the day that her conviction to end her life struck, and retribution for Cain appeared far out of reach, she wondered if she would have taken her revenge if a way to win it had suddenly appeared. She went to the buffet and looked in the mirror, her face appearing behind Ralph and Robert J. Cain. She looked herself in the eye, asked the question again, and realized she had no answer. She looked again because she did know the answer. She didn't see it at first look. She didn't want to. She sighed and squared her shoulders. Ralph had left another fine mess for her to deal with. If Ralph was a doer, then she was an *un*-doer. She had done more than cook for his guests and their spouses. She'd cleaned, too. Once or twice the clean-up required great resourcefulness, even deviousness. As always, she never let him down. The look she saw in her eyes peering over Ralph's ashes said that presented with the chance she would clean this mess just like all the others.

Bobby

III

Twelve months after the Shit Hit the Fan, Bobby felt safe enough to start planning for tomorrows that did not include prison. With the passage of another two months, he planned for a tomorrow with no thought of prison at all. All this time the money was secularly squirreled away quietly and cautiously accrued interest.

Bobby had used his time wisely as an unemployed businessman. He looked for jobs, but with ENCO on his

CV he had little hope of gainful employment. He didn't want a job, but the search was part of his cover. He wanted to be able to say with a hint of panic in both his voice and his eyes that he didn't know what he and his family would do if he couldn't get a job that would support their lifestyle. Giselle did her part to look scared. It was a very sincere effort because she didn't know about the stash. It wasn't that Bobby was going to run off with the dough, but if he told her he had it she would spend it, and that would be noticed. Her pain and mortification at losing their country club membership for failure to pay dues was public and her anger at him was very real. His assurances that things would get better fell on stony distrust. At least in private, he stoically absorbed the blows. As the weeks and months of her abuse accumulated, he decided he didn't care if she was around for the payoff or not. A guy with almost seven million hidden bucks was a good catch for a lot of women.

The first step in his plan with no thought of retribution was to form an LLC with his creative accountant, the only other person who knew about the squirreled away funds. Roadrunner Enterprises RJC could now buy and sell with no overt connection to him. The first thing the LLC bought was the perfect piece of land for Bobby to build a glorious house on, ideal for his children and the new acquaintances that would flock to see him in his dream palace. Part of his strategy when he first foresaw the threat of disaster was to make legitimate investments so he would have something to point at as his source of money while he was *persona non grata* into the business world.

The property was perfectly placed to fit his strategy. It was the best piece around, but it was nowhere near the best of what was available within five miles. Had he bought the best it would have caused a lot of undesired attention, plus the best came with a downside he didn't want to worry about. The land wasn't stable so close to the ocean. On the lake he didn't have to worry about erosion, not to mention there was more sun. Just perfect.

Five months later he and all his new furniture moved in without Giselle, who felt that a small town on the coast with no country club was worse than anything else she could think of. She stayed in the house in town and provided a home for the children, who would spend their whole summer in their father's beautiful home on the lake with a private dock where the Jet Skis would be docked next to the speed-boat.

To Bobby's surprise and gratification, he quickly grew to like the small town. He bought what he needed locally and that included most of the furnishings for the house. The influx of local business was appreciated. His daily routine, unless the rain was too heavy, became to drive around the lake and park in the central business area. He had a favorite coffee shop, Darnelle's Coffee and Crunch, where he stopped each day he came to town. He sipped his white mocha latte and read the paper before he walked and window-shopped. On sunny days he went the extra few blocks to the beach, where he would stroll, with his chin-up, and appreciate his good fortune. His concern that someone would recognize him and cause him grief disappeared.

Life had moved on.

Marcella

IV

She had done all she could. She had reflected, debated internally, and evaluated to build a rational decision. She augmented it with a spiritualism she found foreign, but since once her feet got wet there was no turning back, she wanted to be sure. Then she was.

She got up for what she knew would be the last time. She felt the resolve deep in her heart. She felt stronger than at any recent time.

She showered and did her hair. Put on all clean clothes for no good reason other than it was a very big day for her even if it wasn't for anyone else. It made her think of the bank not sending anyone to take possession of her house. She would mark her passing with the style it deserved. It wasn't because she didn't want to be probed after death in soiled clothes. There would be no body if she joined Nature with the tide going out. She would ride the under-tow into the deep, never to be seen again.

She stared in the mirror. Over the last year her hair had gone from gray to white, and the lines on her face progressed from finely etched to chiseled, but all she needed were money and hope to pull it together again. She noted her calm demeanor. It was a lie. Her stomach churned and her hands shook. With her head she knew what she planned was right, but that didn't play well with the part of her, as it did in all humans, that feared death.

The sun shone in the window and she thought it was far too nice a day to die. Sunshine on the coast was never to be disrespected.

"Get over it!" she said aloud and thought of Crystal Thorgard. The day had come -- or it would come tomorrow -- when Crystal would look next door and not see anyone. "I shall die on a sunny day in all its glory. I shall take it as a tribute to my life. Besides my walk about town on the way to the beach will be delightful."

At ten o'clock she dressed in a coat, hat, and white gloves. With her purse on her arm she examined herself in the hall mirror. The set look on her face might alarm people if she saw someone she knew, so she practiced a smile. Not her best, but it would defuse any concern. She reviewed her plan. An hour to walk her chosen route to reach the beach, no more than an hour and a quarter. When she got there she might have to wait for a few minutes until there was no one to see her as she walked into the waves. The idea of a misbegotten rescue filled her with dread. It was the only thing that would make her change her plan.

Marcella Packer opened her door and stepped out.

Undeterred by the cheery weather, she set off. Her chosen path wound through the neighborhood then over to the main street through town. She nodded at the homes she admired, waved at a few folks out examining the winter damage to their yards. She even chatted briefly with Mark Travis who had recently lost his wife. Marcella had served coffee at the reception in the church hall. She inquired as to how he was getting on.

"You don't know how you're going to miss them until they're gone," he said and a tear came to his eye. "Then you realize all the things you never thanked her for."

She stopped and gave him a supportive smile before saying, "It will get better. You'll adjust. Even do things you never thought you would, or could."

She thought he would be the last person she would talk to. It was the reason she'd said anything at all.

When she reached Highway 101, the main street, she slowed and started her window-shopping. It wasn't clear to her why window-shopping was important. A last stab at normalcy? Keeping up appearances for anyone who might see her? She saw Darnelle's a few windows down and considered a last cup and one of the excellent bear claws Darnelle sold. She had some money and there was no point in saving it. She certainly didn't need to worry about the calories. No, she thought with a shake of her head. She was procrastinating. The tide had already begun the turn. She knew if she walked in at noon the undertow would carry her body far out, never to return.

Even so the temptation of a last indulgence brought saliva to her mouth and a lump to her stomach. She looked in the window to see if there was a line. No line, she told herself, she'll stop. Line, then she would keep moving. She tried to see past the man sitting in the window, but he kept moving as he talked on a cell phone and waved his arms. Selfish beast, she thought. Then he was still.

Her world shook.

She stopped walking, and then backed up a few steps.

She looked through the glass again and her heart stopped.

She blinked her eyes and stared again, but the man had stood and begun walking away.

Marcella walked quickly to the door. She opened it and stepped in to the coffee shop in time to hear the end of an exchange between Darnelle and the man. He laughed and said something over his shoulder as he left. Her ears rang and she couldn't distinguish the words he'd spoken.

She stood rooted to the floor until Darnelle's voice cut through her paralysis.

"Hi, Mrs. Packer! What can I get you today? Those bear claws are just out. Still warm."

Marcella's feet shuffled to the counter.

"Do you know that man?" she asked, pointing vaguely at the door. "He . . . kind of looks familiar."

"Sure. It's Bobby Cain. Nice guy. He's a regular."

"A regular? He lives here?"

"He sure does! He lives in that big new house on the lake. The one with all the gables."

The rush of blood to her head sent her reeling. She staggered, and reached for a chair back, but missed and fell to a knee. Darnelle came running out to catch her before she fell flat. The pounding in Marcella's head blocked all of her senses. The first thing she saw as the black cleared to gray and then to a coastal fog-like field of blurred vision was Darnelle's concerned face staring at her.

"I've called the paramedics," the coffee shop owner said.

Marcella drew a deep breath and shook her head.

"Oh, I'm sorry to be such a bother! I've been a little weak lately, but I don't need any help."

"Don't be silly," Darnelle insisted. "Sit right there."

She returned moments later with black coffee and set it at Marcella's elbow. "Drink this and it will get you righted."

Fortunately, there were no other customers. Marcella took two sips and drew another long breath. Her heart had slowed and her vision seemed almost normal again. Mentally she was as agitated as at any moment in her life. She slowly stood to test her balance and found it only minimally unsteady. She picked up her purse and slowly walked the five steps to the counter.

"Thank you for your kindness," she said as she took two dollars from her purse and laid it next to the cash register.

"Oh, no, Mrs. Packer! On the house. Are you sure you don't want help?"

Marcella grimly smiled and shook her head. "The walk home will do me good. All that fresh air. Please cancel the ambulance. I can't afford it anyway."

With the words out of her mouth Marcella felt stricken. She never shared her business. She blushed furiously and walked as quickly as she could to the door. As it clicked behind her, she looked around. She immediately saw that her world had flipped. The downhill way to the beach now appeared uphill while the road home now seemed the far easier.

Marcella headed for home. By the time she reached it she knew what she had to do.

Her first stop was the mud room. First she checked for clay and the other ingredients for what she planned for her very special piece. She exercised the chains on the hoist. She oiled the mechanism to ensure it would not bind half way through the task at hand. Satisfied she had what she needed, she walked her way through the process. She looked into the kiln again and decided it would take some arranging to fit everything. Next she checked the small chainsaw. She pulled the cord until it caught on the third try. She checked the fuel and felt sure she had enough.

Inside the house she took her sketch pad to the dining room table and opened it to a blank page. She stared at the paper and imagined what would look the best. There was a lot of pressure to make it just right. It had to look nice on the buffet next to Ralph. She smiled. The idea of the two of them side by side appealed to her. The symmetry felt right with the universe.

She made a few random sketches and discarded them with hardly a second look. She thumbed through the old drawings until she found the ones she'd done for Ralph's urn. She reviewed them with looks to the buffet. The reason she liked Ralph's was that it didn't look like an urn with the remains of a human being inside. It was done in a similar style to her other pieces in the living room and kitchen. She wanted the new piece to go hand in hand, so to speak, with Ralph's.

She stopped to make tea and cleanse her mind. She had always found that creating on a cluttered mind left her with nothing but disappointment. She sipped her

Earl Grey, not the decaffeinated variety but the real thing, until she felt refreshed.

Six hours later she had a full color drawing of exactly what she needed. She smiled and thanked the universe, frowning at the thought. It was the second time that day she'd invoked the universe. She didn't remember ever doing that before.

She walked out the front door into a clear and crisp February night. A sliver of a new moon hung to the south and a quarter of the way above the horizon.

A new moon.

A new beginning.

Afterword

After the discovery of the clothes on the beach, the sheriff's second out of the ordinary incident was a phone call from the wife of a new resident gone missing. It came on the third day after Marcella Packer had apparently walked into the Pacific. At first there was no reason to think the two were related.

The caller said her name was Mrs. Giselle Cain and she lived in Portland. Her husband, Robert J. Cain, had just built a house in town and spent most of his time there. No, they weren't separated. It just worked better this way. She didn't elaborate and Fredericks moved back to the issue at hand. She said that her husband had not been heard from in five days.

"How often did he usually call?" the sheriff asked.

"Usually every day. At least once. Sometimes three or four times."

"He never missed a day?"

"Sure, every now and then, but it was rare. Never two days in a row."

"And he didn't say anything about going anywhere?"

"Oh, for Christ's sake!" Mrs. Cain said her exasperation clear. "No. I am not an idiot."

"Are you implying you suspect foul play?"

"Can you send someone to the house to see if anything is wrong? We pay a lot of property taxes. I don't think it's too much to ask."

"I will do that. In fact, I'll go myself. Nothing but the best for a prime property tax-payer. What's the address?"

She hesitated. He thought she was working on a snappy come-back to his sarcasm.

"I don't know," she finally said. "It's new. You can't miss it. It's that new one on the lake with all the gables."

Fredericks knew the house like everyone else anywhere near the lake. "I'll call you after I check. Is this the best number?"

She said it was and hung up.

The extended dry weather meant he could go around the south end of the lake, a choice often not available during the winter because of flooding.

He'd noticed the house often on his rounds. For a place that was so visible from the waterside, the road side was pretty well shielded by laurel hedges. The garage and the driveway that would hold at least six cars were easy to see. The house not so much. Fredericks parked the cruiser in the driveway. He walked to the front door and knocked. No answer. He knocked again and then tried the door knob.

It opened. He sighed and took the holster strap off his weapon. He checked to be sure it sat loose so he could get it out if necessary. Then he pushed the door open.

He entered. A home security panel blinked on the wall, but it was not engaged. He walked slowly through the house. Aside from a chair on its side in the dining room, he found nothing amiss. On a kitchen counter he found an open bottle of beer and the fixings for a cup of tea. Earl Grey, he noticed.

He walked up-stairs. As he did and looked around he wondered how much this place had cost. He'd heard a couple of million and so far he'd seen nothing to make him doubt that heady number. Bedrooms and two bathrooms were the first rooms he entered. At the end of the hall he found a large study or office and then a huge bedroom suite with a walkthrough bathroom. In one of the closets he found a wall safe with the door open. Nothing inside.

He sighed again. He reached for his phone and called Gloria at the office. He asked her to get Giselle Cain on and to be sure and record the call. A minute later he had Mrs. Cain.

"I found your front door closed but unlocked. Does that sound like your husband, ma'am?"

"No, Bobby was very security conscious. Was the alarm set?"

"No, Ma'am. There was a chair on its side in the dining room. The rest of the house looks undisturbed with one exception. The wall safe is open upstairs. It's empty."

"Oh, my god!" Giselle Cain cried. "I warned him!"

Fredericks clenched his teeth, determined to stay his course.

"Do you know what he would have kept in it?"

"Cash. Bearer bonds."

"How much?"

"I don't know. At least a million dollars. Maybe more."

"A million! How come so much?" Giselle Cain hesitated so long he had to prompt her. "We're following through here and can use any help. What we're seeing so far is serious."

"He was one of the Fish in a Barrel guys," Giselle said. "He was paranoid someone would recognize him and he might have to take a fast extended vacation."

Fredericks knew the term. He also knew the misery the raid on his town's seniors had caused.

"Not too smart a place for your husband to build."

"I told him, but he liked it there. He said enough time had passed."

"The safe sort of contradicts that."

"That was Bobby. What's next?"

"We put out a wide BOLO and see if we can find him. I'll keep you informed."

"Off the record, Sheriff. What do you think?"

"I don't think off the record. I'll call you when we have something." He hung up.

He didn't think out loud about any case, but as he looked into the empty safe he thought things looked bleak for Bobby Cain.

* * * * *

With a break in the off-season flurry of crime, Fredericks looked into the missing Bobby Cain. The sheriff had always fancied himself a detective, and here was a chance to detect. In a couple of hours, he discovered that Cain had been a creature of habit. He usually took a stroll around town on dry days, and even some when it rained but didn't pour. Fredericks visited the stores and shops on Cain's route. He eventually reached Darnelle's.

"Sure, Bobby Cain's a regular. He hasn't been around for a few days. Anything wrong?"

"Can't say yet. He say anything about going away?"

"Not a word."

"Anything out of the ordinary happen with him?"

Darnelle thought for a moment. "Marcella Packer asked about him."

A seismic rattle shook his old cop cynicism. "When?"

"I'd guess a day or two before he stopped coming in."

"Why'd she ask?"

"It was odd. She acted like she'd seen a ghost. I thought she was going to faint. I brought her a cuppa and called the paramedics. She turned them both down. She said something out of character, though."

"What?"

"She was always so private. Never said a word about herself. She told me to cancel the call for the paramedics because she couldn't afford them. It was odd because everybody has insurance, don't they?"

He drove back to his office. He stopped at the front desk and asked Gloria about Marcella Packer.

"Sure, she's in our church. You know that, Sheriff."

"Yeah, but I've only talked to her a couple of times. Weren't you on a committee or something with her?"

"Several, why?"

"What happened to her? How'd she lose her money?"

"She didn't! It was that wild man husband of hers with his get rich quick ideas. He invested in some bad stocks and lost it all. Then the bastard died."

"Any idea which stocks?" he asked, while the cynicism rattled louder.

"I do. He was one of the ones that got picked clean by those Fish in a Barrel guys."

Fredericks turned and walked to the door.

"Going out, Sheriff?" Gloria asked.

"Marcella Packer's. Time to take a closer look."

"That Cain fella? Fish in a Barrel?"

"Maybe."

Twenty minutes later with the setting sun throwing long shadows on the Packers yard, Fredericks took a closer look. He started outside. He looked in the garage. A car sat there just as one would expect with its owner having taken a walk into the Pacific Ocean. He took the keys he'd picked up on his last visit and opened the trunk. Cluttered mostly with what he assumed were potting supplies, but nothing suspicious. He closed it and poked around the garage finding nothing to raise an eyebrow.

He went to the shed. He saw the kiln attached to the structure. He remembered talking to her about her potting in one of those rare conversations. He liked her pieces.

He opened the mud-room. Two minutes later he called Gloria again.

"Tell Gordon to get over here to the Packer place. Tell him to bring the crime scene kit with two bottles of Luminol and the light."

Fredericks took a slower look through Marcella Packer's house. No surprise that it was neat and clean, just like he always saw her. The dining room table was the only mess. Papers were scattered all over the top. He also found a folder with papers that all seemed to pertain to her eviction. He looked at the dates and then searched his memory. She'd asked him about evictions well before she got the letter they'd found in her pocket. Marcella was a planner. In the sheriff's experience, planners didn't commit suicide. It admitted a failure to find a better plan.

He recognized her more recent Raku pieces and others done a few years back. The glazes were bright and the pieces lighter in form and application. He wondered if her husband had admired her work. At a glance he didn't think so. A shame. It wasn't like Fredericks was an art critic, but he knew what he liked. He also knew that Lucille, the woman who ran the craft and cultural center, always had a piece of Marcella's on display. The pieces weren't for sale, Lucille said, which was a shame. They would sell. When the sheriff asked, Lucille said it was as if Marcella didn't believe in herself.

Fredericks heard a car out front and saw his deputy arrive. They met outside the shed.

"What do we got?" Gordon asked.

"We're lucky it hasn't rained much in the last few weeks. Spray the hoist chain, the sides of the kiln, and then the ground at the door of the shed."

"Good thing you said to bring two bottles of Luminol. That's a lot of spraying."

The implication of the instruction sank in for Gordon.

"Jesus! Are you saying somebody got killed and stashed in the kiln?"

"Just spray and then we'll figure it out!" Fredericks said with his irritation showing.

After the deputy sprayed, the sheriff held the light. He turned it on. This close to dusk the blue light of the chemical's reaction with blood shone brightly.

"That's a lot of blood!" Gordon exclaimed.

"Do inside the shed. Start with the floor near the door. There's a chainsaw on a bench. That might be blood on the teeth so hit it, too."

Gordon put the bag down and stared slack-jawed at the sheriff.

"Are you kidding me? Old Marcella Packer cuts somebody up with a chainsaw and uses them for fire wood in her pottery cooker? No way."

"Gordon! For the last time. Just do the damn job. Besides, if she put someone in the kiln it wouldn't be for firewood. It would be more like cremating them."

His mind flashed to the covered vases on the buffet in the dining room.

"Shit! I'll be back."

Fredericks ran into the house. He stood in the door way to the dining room, pulled on his latex gloves, and stared at what could easily be urns. Both pieces were Raku, so their finishes were dull, but one definitely looked newer than the other. He stood at the buffet and lifted the lids on both pieces. One was fuller than the other.

He'd seen human ashes before, and the contents of the two urns sure looked like human remains. He knew the cremation process destroyed all DNA, so that wouldn't be any help. He called the office.

"Hey, Gloria, how long ago did Marcella's husband die?"

"I don't know, Sheriff. Two years ago; something like that."

"Did she have him cremated?"

"She did. Made the urn herself, too. I remember when she showed us at the church. It was real nice. None of us had ever thought of such a thing, not that we could have done anything about it if we had. Got to have a kiln. She has a nice one. Pretty big, too."

"Thanks, Gloria."

"I'm going home in a couple of minutes, Sheriff. You need anything? You want me to stay?"

"No, thanks, Gloria. Go on home. What we have will still be here tomorrow."

Fredericks looked again into the urns. The one on the right had to be her husband. The whole thing, ashes too, seemed older. He couldn't say why, but they did. So that left the question as to who was in the newer one. Even with his gloves on he was loathe to sift the grit through his hands, but he did wonder why one was fuller than the other. He took a breath and dug around. He felt something bigger in the middle. His fingers explored the shape and his brain registered the feel.

"Son of a bitch!" he said aloud as he lifted a spent slug out of the urn. The slug was black from the fire and slightly misshapen, but it was a spent round.

"The DA is not going to like this," he said, as he dropped the slug back in the urn with the ashes.

He decided to leave Gordon on-site tomorrow. He knew where he'd be. He'd be in Newport laying it out for District Attorney Thomas Hazelton.

* * * * *

Hazelton had wanted a court recorder to be in the room along with a deputy DA, but Fredericks suggested they talk alone first.

Twenty minutes later Hazelton stared across his desk before looking down at his notes.

"Let me get this straight. Or as straight as it gets. You got a nice old lady that the whole town liked and felt sorry for because she was getting tossed out of her house after her husband, now deceased, lost it all to one of those Fish in a Barrel guys that coincidentally moves in across the lake from her. So far so good?"

"On the money," Fredericks said.

"Now we get to the hard part. The way you see it, the old lady spots the guy that destroyed her and her husband's life while she was out for a walk. So she somehow finds the guy – pardon my straightforward narration here minus the question marks – shoots the guy, steals a million bucks, miraculously gets him back to her house and into the back-yard where she cuts him up with a chainsaw into hunks that fit in her kiln, incinerates him, and dumps his ashes into a homemade urn and puts it in the dining room next to her departed husband's ashes whose death she had nothing to do with, and then walks into the sea. That about right?"

Fredericks shrugged. "That is one way it could have happened."

"I don't think I can take plan B right now."

Fredericks ignored the plea. "What happened to the money and the bearer bonds?" he asked. "Plus, we found Ralph Packer's passport but not Marcella's. If it weren't for the neat stack of her clothes on the beach where we couldn't help but find them, we wouldn't even be thinking she was dead."

"So the pop version of that one," Hazelton said, "is the sweet old lady kills the scumbag that stole all her money and then disappears to the South Seas to live off it. That one plays a lot better."

"Only because you didn't mention the chainsaw and the kiln."

The district attorney turned to look out the window. He shrugged his shoulders and turned back.

"I don't see a real good way to spin that part," he said. "Maybe they become crime scene details withheld to weed out false confessions."

Fredericks stared at Hazelton, who waved the idea off. Not the withholding, but the idea there would be false confessions.

"You do see we don't have any bodies, right?" Sheriff Fredericks said.

"That's a whole different story. We might be looking for someone who may be dead for killing someone that may not be dead. Or something like that." Hazelton held up a finger. "Not to mention this guy Cain was hated by a whole bunch of people, many of whom lived near where this nut job decides to build an audacious new house where he can rub their noses in it."

The two men sat there in silence. Fredericks spoke first.

"What do you want me to do? I've got people asking around town about Marcella."

Hazelton leaned back in his chair before saying, "Let's say she killed him, did all the rest of it too, and took his money which is cash and good as. How much of a head start does she have?"

"Four or five days. At least. We could look for a trail. I mean, how did she get out of town? That's where to start."

Hazelton stood and walked to a framed picture hanging on the wall. It was a shot of his last election victory party.

"I am an elected official sworn to pursue and prosecute the criminals of Lincoln County. The people who vote for me trust me to use my discretion to find the best way to do this. Sometimes 'discretion' and 'pursue and prosecute' don't always see eye to eye. This is one of those times."

He returned to his desk. He straightened his suit coat before he sat, and after he took his seat he leaned forward with his hands folded on his desk.

"If we had some bodies it would be easier, but we don't. That said, here's the way I see it. It will be easy to pass on a nebulous pursuit of a woman with the approval rating of Mrs. Santa Claus for perhaps committing a crime on a man reviled by most who knew him."

Hazelton remained leaning back.

"Carl, let me ask you this." Fredericks knew Hazelton only used his first name when they were off the record. "Is your heart really up for a search for Marcella Packer? We'd use a hunk of our limited funds on what could well be a fool's errand. Wouldn't you rather just imagine she's sitting on a distant beach under an umbrella sipping a mai tai?"

*   *   *   *   *

February's False Spring had ended during the meeting. As Sheriff Carl Fredericks drove north for the twenty miles between Newport and Lincoln City, the wind blew rain in sheets sideways across the highway.

Things were back to normal.

To End with . . .

Fifty-two days after the meeting in Newport, three days after Easter, Carl Fredericks received a small package in the mail postmarked New Orleans. Inside, he found a cocktail umbrella suitable for an exotic drink. There was also a note.

Disregard postmark. MP.

ACE

A rugged and battle-scarred ex-GI, named Daniel Thomas Spader, or Dan T to his friends, and Ace to those who know the story of his intimate tattoo, roams the streets of Island City looking for a killer. The characters Dan T meets on his search have all had miraculous escapes from death, many in the recently concluded World War II. Versions of the story become so common and echo his own, that Dan T sees a new mystery with far greater implications. Add the disturbing sense of having done it all before, and Dan T's search becomes an existential journey in search of transcendence while answers to traditional questions fade into the prevailing mist of Island City.

Light many lamps and gather round his bed.
Lend him your eyes, warm blood, and will to live.
Speak to him; rouse him; you may save him yet.
He's young; he hated War; how should he die
When cruel old campaigners win safe through?

But death replied: 'I choose him.' So he went,
And there was silence in the summer night;
Silence and safety; and the veils of sleep.
Then, far away, the thudding of the guns.

From *The Death Bed*

SIEGFRIED SASSOON, 1916

"The meaning of life is that it stops."

FRANZ KAFKA

ACE HIGH by Ken Byers

FROM THE LIGHT AND MIST

"Daniel Thomas Spader.   Daniel Thomas Spader.   Daniel Thomas Spader. Daniel Thomas Spader."

The soft, distant voices grew louder and then stopped before they came close. I faded once again.

I swam not in water. Viscous, like an embryonic fluid. The calling of my name long gone as the fluid swept me away. Swept away on a current from no place I knew and dropped in a place unknown. I curled inward. Lost.

Time passed. Perhaps a great deal of time. I thought of trees growing until tall and thick, limbs groaning under the weight of snow. Like the snow that fell the day the bullets stitched my back. The day I died. The day the light and mist drew me in.

If the light and mist mean death, what am I now? All I had were questions. The voices returned, once again summoning me.

I opened my eyes. I awakened on the first day of this life.

The phone rang.

Chapter 1

I jumped off the streetcar's foot board and blended with the lunch crowd that packed the sidewalks. It was mostly men in coveralls and dirty skull-tight work caps smudged black from the mills and foundries. Me in my rumpled suit stood out. Tall, at six-foot-two and battled scared, made me standout even more. Inside Giga's Saloon I pushed toward the counter and met Virgil Wozinsky's eyes in the mirror behind the bar. He elbowed the man to his right off the stool.

"Welcome back, Ace," he said. "I been saving it."

The counterman poured coffee in my cup.

"Thanks, Mike," I said.

Louise, the barmaid, waved as Woozy lit a Chesterfield.

"This had better be good," I said to my old partner. "I just got to sleep when the phone rang."

"Yeah, you look like you just got out of a coffin."

"Good-bye, unless there are reasons beyond insults to stay."

"It'll pay your rent for another day or two, although why you live in that dump I'll never know. If you had a real job you wouldn't be out all night."

"I've always worked nights."

"Yeah, but now you ain't even working. Join the world. Get a place with a private shitter. Get some chairs; invite people over. Go all out."

"There's nothing wrong with my place."

"The place is a firetrap!" He coughed on inhaled smoke. "It's on the fourth floor, for Christ's sake. What are you going to do in a fire? I thought you were afraid of fire."

"You have to confront your fears."

"Glad to hear it. You'll love this case, then."

"I'm tired. I want to go back to sleep."

"Lots of time to sleep when you're dead. Besides, you should be well rested."

I drank my coffee and watched him in the mirror.

"Where's Pugh?" I asked, Jessie Pugh being his latest partner.

"Probably home in bed where I oughta be," Woozy answered. "We got swing this week. That's how come I know what I'm about to dump on ya'."

"Which is what?"

"A colored floater out in Mock Bottom."

I pushed off the stool and took a couple of quarters out of my pocket.

"Sit down, Ace."

"You know I don't do coloreds."

"I thought you were a little more open-minded than that."

"What is this? You get me up for a job you know I won't take? I can't take a colored case by myself, and my open mind ain't the problem."

He hunched forward on his stool. "Didn't you just say you have to confront your fears?"

I stared at his back. "This about going back to the Spew."

"It's more about you gotta get back on the horse," the old soldier said.

"Without a badge nobody's going to talk to me in the Spew," I said, dancing around the real issue.

"That part of town ain't no different than anywhere else in paradise," Woozy said, joining the dance. "They'll talk to you if you have a badge, sure, but they're lying if their lips are moving. Lousy excuse, Ace. This is a chance to get back to where you got shot."

At last. He sidled up to the point. I sat down again and drank coffee.

"Maybe," I finally said. "Why do you want me back in the Spew? Who's the corpse?"

I didn't have the guts to pursue the real topic, and pulled back into the old do-si-do.

"Kid named Melvin Jackson."

"You're working a race case?"

"The father's got some clout."

I pushed my hat back and took a sip.

"Used to be an oxymoron."

"Things are changing, Dan T. Maybe not fast, but they're changing. A few blacks came out of W-W-Two with some station. Joshua Jackson, the father, was one of them. Came out a major. Won some decorations and went into business. He invented something they use in Pullman cars. Now he's rich enough to get City Hall's attention."

"So if you're a Negro and got money, you get heard."

"Money's color blind. We got all kinds in Island City now. Coloreds, Chinks, you name it."

"Polacks," I added.

"Yeah, even Polacks. But some things don't change. We got some heavy flak on this Jackson hit. Somebody don't want us doing what we're supposed to be doing."

"Who?" I asked. "Why?"

"Don't know. Captain Yes-sir called us off, but he ain't even making it look good. Pugh called in from a box and got the word. Drop it. Do it now and shut up. Real subtle."

"So being good little soldiers, you did."

"Not without some spunk, though!" he shrugged, indicating he was here talking to me which amounted to an open act of defiance. "We'd been working a new lead, but Pugh didn't even have a chance to tell him. I called back and tried, but Captain Asshole hung up on me. End of song. But, you know Pinella's never done one damn thing on his own."

Gino Pinella, Captain Yes-sir, came by the name honestly.

"What'd you find that got your back up? Ah, ha!" I spun on the stool to face him. "Here comes the hook!"

"Yeah, this is it. Melvin, my floater, was twenty-four, bright like his old man, and a hit with the ladies. We already knew that. What we didn't know till last night was who he was currently hitting it off with. But it ain't no aha. It's more like an oh-oh."

"Cut to it."

He bounced a fresh pack of Chesterfields on the bar, then tore off the cellophane.

"It's the Judge's one and only – Christina. She's back after Daddy got her off for being juiced and driving her Caddie convertible over a kid."

I knew this, and he knew I did. He was giving me time to think.

"You might remember the Judge found a fall guy and she walked," he said. "She's been seeing Jackson for at least a month."

Wozinsky let his unlit smoke dangle in the corner of his mouth.

"Sounds like Pinella was a little slow shutting you down," I said.

"We worked it for three days."

"Long time if somebody wanted to kill it."

"It takes a while for shit to flow up hill. Maybe the Judge wasn't ready to believe his kid was going out with a colored."

"Maybe. What about the Jackson family?"

"Pugh and me talked to the father right after we had the ID. After that he called the station every night at midnight. He got madder 'n hell when I told him we'd been called off."

"How'd you leave it?"

"I told him you'd be calling." He reached into an inside pocket and pulled out a slip of paper and set it on the counter between us. "The number. I told him if he wants to settle the bill on his son, he should deal with you."

"That all you said?"

Woozy finished his coffee and signaled for more. Louise brought the pot and filled both our cups.

"No." He finally lit the smoke, took a drag, and picked tobacco off his tongue. "I told him you got results and he shouldn't worry about how."

Woozy had an Old Testament view of the world and the law. The guilty had to pay even if it meant an end run.

I used a fingernail to flick the paper with Jackson's number. "The Masked Avenger rides again, eh?"

He coughed, and swiveled his stool.

"What do you want, Ace? You ain't the same since you died."

At last.

"I didn't die. What do you think I want?"

"Gut check. You want a gut check to be sure you ain't dead." He pinched my arm and shrugged. "I got to do that when I see you."

"I did not die. You don't believe in ghosts and neither do I."

68

"You were a bad fit as a cop, Ace. Cops ain't soldiers, which you was good at. But here, you don't get to blast the bad guys just because you got a gun in your hand. It sucks, I know, but it's the way."

"The war was a long time ago."

"Not yours," he said. "Man, you gotta face the truth. You should'a left the Judge's wife alone."

He'd had enough of the "dead" question. So had I.

"Hildy had nothing to do with it," I told him.

"Yes she did." He took a big swig on his coffee and made a face. "The word went out. My man Ace dead as a busted flush. Dead on the floor in Birdlegs's office. Dead at the hands of two guys conveniently dead themselves. Then guess what? You ain't dead. How come, I asked? Everybody shrugs. You just ain't dead. You got the holes in you that oughta mean dead, but," he thumped my chest, "you ain't fucking dead! Not that I'm complaining. I woulda missed you."

"I'm not afraid to die."

"So what's that gotta do with the price of tea in China? I know you, Ace. You're afraid of fire. You're afraid of the dark. You're afraid to go swimming. You got more fears than an asylum."

"I had a bad war."

"Every swinging dick who fought and lived had a bad war. As long as you're asking, I'll tell you what else I think. You didn't die because you're not afraid of dying. You don't get to die for good until you survive fire, the dark, and drowning. One day, after all that, I'll pinch your arm and you won't be there."

I ignored him.

"You gotta come up with an answer here, Ace. Without death, what's the point of God?"

I looked at Joshua Jackson's phone number on the paper.

"Come on. Call the man," Woozy said, after I sigh. "You didn't just get off the boat. You're a genius with this kind of case."

It wasn't like Woozy to lather and stir.

"Come on, Dan T. Set your foot on the path. This is about right and wrong, Birdlegs and the Judge. It's about Hildy Bell and her strange daughter. Hell, it's Island City our home, sweet, home."

He pushed the paper closer to me, then tapped it with his finger. I knew I was going to do it.

"Let's go look at the crime scene," I said.

We vacated our stools leaving behind only questions that neither of us wanted to answer.

Chapter 2

The founders of Island City used their imagination to make money. They hadn't wasted it on names for either the town or the streets. The river still used its native name of Nah-Neek-Na. South of town it broke into the East branch and the West branch giving Island City the appearance of existing in the crotch of a lopsided slingshot. North of town, the East fork wrapped around the top and met the West fork at the northwest corner. The Calder Hills, so named for the town's first tycoon, formed the keel of the lower town like an aircraft carrier turned turtle. Between the river and the hills, centuries of erosion left five or six miles of flood plain that periodically did just that in the spring runoffs surrounding higher ground. Everybody got wet, but it was the rich who sold boats to the rest of us.

Mock Bottom, so named because it had no real bottom, made up the near shore of the East branch. It was nothing more than silt washed into a catch basin by mighty floods. Every year the runoffs, even the ones that didn't flood, stirred the silt and added viscosity to the water so detritus floated instead of sank. If you wanted to lose a body it was a dumb place to dump it. The basin also captured trees washed into the runoff-fed current, which bobbed and rubbed against the shoreline like rough sandpaper.

Woozy parked on the street that ran along the crest of the embankment. He opened the trunk of his city cruiser, took out two pair of waders and handed me one.

"They'll fit," he said. "I kept your old ones just in case."

The crime scene was long gone. No sawhorses, no beat cop rocking on his heels, no sign that a murdered body had been found. I wondered if that meant it had never happened. When we got closer to the water I saw signs of heavy feet stomping the soggy ground. The dead body slowly appeared in my imagination.

"Medical examiner have any insight?" I asked.

"Death by drowning. Brilliant. Anything beyond that never got done."

"Harry Lieberman still doing the cutting?"

"Yeah. I called and he told me the body got pulled so fast he hadn't had time to sharpen a knife."

"Pulled?"

"Yeah, pulled. I thought he meant it as a euphemism, but the body literally got pulled. There one minute and then *poof.*"

"Gone?"

"Like a fart in the wind!"

"How'd his father take that?"

"Haven't told him. Thought you'd like the pleasure."

"Why haven't you told him, for Christ's sake?"

"Because I haven't talked to him! It takes a couple of days before Harry does an autopsy unless it's a rush. This wasn't. Then it was."

"What a way to start! What do you want me to do?"

"Tell me where the body entered the water. You know this river better than most."

I looked up the hill. No sign of anything heavy rolling down.

"How much did the kid weigh?"

"Wiry. About one-fifty."

"What was he wearing?"

"Street clothes."

I looked across the dead and blackening trees stuck on their sides in the primordial soup of the catch basin. The river flowed from right to left, the current no closer than two hundred yards to the shore. The shipyards lay around the point to the left, the city and its waterfront to the right. The far sides of North River lay under a heavy cloud cover that came down to the deck. All I could see was a vague suggestion of trees and hillside.

"He got dumped from a boat," I said.

"How'd he make it to shore across the snags?"

"He didn't. All this floating shit swings back and forth in the current. The body found a gate and sailed on in like a sneak attack. Usually, if a boat dumps it out far enough, the current takes it away. The killers were unlucky. Who found it?"

"A guy walking his dog. Said the dog almost ripped his arm out of its socket dragging him down the hill. What kind of boat?"

"One with a motor. The current's too fast to row."

"Boat with a motor is a lot of trouble," he said. "Maybe they didn't care if it got found."

"No, they cared. No body, no case. Sure, they got the case closed, but it cost somebody."

"Maybe they didn't know what they were doing," he said.

"That's possible. Good at killing, bad at hiding. Why don't you look for the boat and the strings, and I'll see Jackson."

"I'm off the case."

"And I can't be on it. We got a better chance than most."

The street names in Island City bore numbers east and west, and letters north and south. Hard to get lost, and even harder to feel any esthetic connection.

Joshua Jackson lived on "J" street between Twenty-Third and Twenty-Fourth, North. This put it on Swamp Isle, a section drained fifteen years ago during the public works explosion before World War II. Of course it wasn't called Swamp Isle anymore. The new name was Water View Inlet, although the water had been pumped out well before the christening, and the view was across Mock Bottom. Still, it was an uppity neighborhood if you were colored, and painful if your view included where your son had been murdered.

I parked in front of the Jackson house, turned the key off, and waited for the engine to die. It took longer each time. I never popped the clutch to put it out of its misery, instead I listened to it burp and cough, and thought about death. I should have died there on the floor in the backroom of the Lullaby. The bullets had gone in. They made holes in me and my life ran out. I'd been shot before. In the war. It was Belgium in winter. Bullets went in, I ran out. I should have died then, too. I'd seen men die with less. Both times I'd lain there losing consciousness knowing I was dying. I felt bad both times because I had no pithy summation of my years, and without grave insight my life felt meaningless. I'd come; I'd died. The car burped into silence without a final thought either.

I'd called Jackson so he knew I was coming. I walked through a large yard that fronted the house and gave it a sharper look than the rest of the houses on the street.

Joshua Jackson answered my knock so fast he must have been waiting in the entry way. He stood tall and distinguished with puffs of gray like scattered clouds in his otherwise short black hair. He wore a thin moustache with a gray southbound stripe under his nose. I shook the hand he offered. He led me into the library. The room wasn't big, but he'd made the most of it. Books lined three walls, broken only by a suggestion of a window covered with heavy drapes. The fourth wall held a fireplace. Above the mantel hung a painting of Jesus, complete with halo and rising sun. A desk took up a corner. Facing leather chairs bookmarked a small table with a chessboard one move into a new game. A small desk light fought a losing battle with the dark.

After he had us seated in the leather chairs separated by the chessboard, he said, "I don't understand Sargent Wozinsky's description of what you do."

Even though his voice came out low and smooth, he had himself on a tight rein. The red lines in his eyes said he hadn't been sleeping, and he had a difficult time sitting still.

"I used to be in the department."

"So Sargent Wozinsky said, but what did he mean by you'd be harder to stop?"

"I'm not official. I work for you. You can fire me, but if I'm working for you there's only one other way to call me off."

Jackson's squirming stopped with my last words. He briefly met my eyes, and then looked away as my meaning sank in.

"He said you get results -- even go outside the law."

"Sometimes the law is — limited. I look for alternatives. Sometimes they aren't pleasant, or even legal. But they're always appropriate."

"An eye for an eye? Isn't that taking the law," a pause and a glance at the portrait of Jesus, "into your own hands?"

"Not the law in the books. Something more fundamental."

Jackson could sit no longer. He stood and began pacing.

"Is it usually parents that hire you?"

"I don't give references."

"I know, I know," he said, stopping with his back to me and his hands folded where I could see them. "This is difficult. My great-grandparents were slaves in South Carolina. They escaped to Chicago during the Civil War. That was a long time ago."

He rocked back and forth on his heels.

"Here I am, the only one out of fourteen children to have a college education. Isn't that amazing? Only in America." He paused, shaking his head. "I fought to defend this country. Wounded. I thought I'd died."

He sighed, and then rubbed his face.

"I know nothing is perfect," he said, turning. "My people still have a long way to go, but even so, it's better than what it would be anywhere else. I believe that. But I can't accept my son being murdered."

He started pacing again.

"Melvin and I weren't close. I tried to show him that a man of color could be successful with things the way they are. But he didn't want to do it my way. He had his own ideas, and we argued. Now he's dead, and I feel like I failed him. His murder must be dealt with. If it isn't, then he was right. I don't want to let him down again."

Joshua Jackson's voice broke. When he regained control, he walked to a wooden dais near his desk. He lifted a Bible and waved it at me.

"'Vengeance is mine, saith the Lord'" He stopped talking and his chin touched his chest. He sighed, and gave it another try. "'Vengeance is mine, saith the Lord.' By hiring you, Mr. Spader, I am condemning my soul to Hell. So be it. Tell the killers I'll see them there. Give them the message. Please."

"I can't promise yet. If I can, I'll take the job."

"What will you do first?"

"I'll ask you some questions – a few will hurt."

"Ask your questions."

"Did you know your son was seeing Christina Bell?"

Jackson hadn't known until a week before his son disappeared. When he found out, he was upset. He told his son he was asking too much of the girl's family. The way he said it made it clear it was too much for him as well.

He gave me some background and a short list of Melvin's friends. Because Melvin had turned his back on school and the family business, his parents knew very little. None of the jobs his father knew of lasted. The boy was smart, but refused to acknowledge some doors remained closed. The jobs he could get pissed him off and the jobs he couldn't fed his anger. He kept knocking on all those closed doors and it annoyed people. His father saw the frustration and renewed his offer for his son to join the family business, but Melvin again said no. Joshua Jackson said he'd been worried even before the disappearance. That was why he reported it so promptly when Melvin didn't keep an invitation to dinner. His son would never miss a free meal, even if it came with a sermon.

"One more question," I said.

"This the one that hurts?"

"I'm sure they've all hurt, but, yes. Melvin's body is missing from the morgue. Did you authorize moving it?"

Jackson's jaw dropped. He stood even straighter.

"They took his body?" he asked.

"Did you arrange for his body to be moved?"

"Absolutely not."

He dropped his face into his hands and the tears flowed.

Chapter 3

After sleeping through the afternoon and early evening, I left my wreck in the downtown garage and took the streetcar from Chinatown through the tunnel into the Spew. The tunnel dated back to the end of the previous century and was built with Chinese labor, mostly descendants of the people who'd built the transcontinental railroad. Chinatown hugged the waterfront in old buildings in which safes were built into walls above the high-water mark, and ladders came out in the spring. The first signs of spring weren't tulips or daffodils or even skunk cabbage, but the ladders snugged up to the safes.

If the tunnel brought the Chinese to Island City, the shipyards to fight W-W-Two brought the Negroes. Before the war, the Spew was landfill made up of dynamited rock from the bore for the tunnel, and other Island City construction projects. With the war, it was the perfect place for shipyards and housing for the workers. The shipyards were gone, but the people weren't.

The Spew was Island City's version of the ghetto. It was also the septic field for the hills of the rich that pinned the Spew against East River. The rich didn't have to look at the Spew. All their houses at the top either faced the lights of downtown, or the cloud-shrouded far side, but when they flushed the water level rose beneath them.

The Spew, like any subculture, had its king. Moses "Birdlegs" Greer made his office out of the back room of the Lullaby Club, a bar that thrived on the second floor above a boarded-up storefront. I climbed the stairs and suffered the glares of black faces who weren't used to seeing blue eyes in the middle of the week. Whites might cross the line to the Lullaby for the music on a weekend, but they never came on Tuesday.

I didn't recognize the bartender, but that was no surprise. It had been awhile and the last time I was here, I was busy getting shot.

"Birdlegs in?" I asked.

"Who wants to know?"

"Tell him Ace wants a shot of the good stuff."

He checked me out before he finally turned away and went through a door in the back. When he returned, he threw a thumb over his shoulder. As I passed through the backroom door, I felt a breeze ripple through my mind like the ghost of a distant memory, or maybe like I just stepped on my own grave.

The last time I'd seen Birdlegs I lay in the doorway bleeding out. Birdlegs stood over me smiling and holding a still smoking .45 automatic.

At three hundred pounds and shoulders that defied anything off the rack, Birdlegs Greer was a monster. He preferred laughing to scowling, and his high-pitched squeal was one of his trademarks. But don't ever take his toothy grin for benign. He'd ordered men killed while the angelic smile never wavered. Other than the desk Birdlegs sat behind, the room held two plain wooden chairs, a couch covered by a quilt, and a floor lamp with a rip in its shade. Nothing hung on the walls.

"Well, if it ain't the man with the taa-too on his dare-ee-air! You come by after all this time to pay your gratitude bill?"

Birdlegs thought the tattoo of the ace of spades on my ass – a souvenir of a bender before I shipped out to war – was funnier than hell. He always said he wanted one just like it. His dark eyes sparkled and his grin revealed white teeth too small for the rest of his face.

"The way I remember it I saved your ass," I answered.

"Let's look at the facts. You lying there bleeding all over my rug while the two guys that did you are laying right over there," Birdlegs pointed at a spot on the floor, "dead to dyin' thanks to me."

"Back it up about five seconds. I come through the door while those two," I pointed to the same spot, "have the drop on you. They decide to shoot me because I'm a cop and that gives you time to shoot them."

"I woulda got 'em. Didn't need no help."

"Fastest draw in town, right?"

"Wanna see it again?" he laughed, hands still on his desk.

He hadn't stood when I entered. That was another trademark. Other than to shoot people he rarely got out of his chair because his skinny little legs struggled with their load. Hence the name. But he didn't have to move to be a king, and not much happened in his empire that escaped him.

He pulled a good bottle of sour mash, the only one in the whole bar, out of a drawer along with a clean glass. He filled it and the glass that was already sitting on the desk. I took mine and sat down.

"We even," he said. "We'll start a new tab."

We held our glasses up, and drank.

"So what's the news, Ace?"

"I'd appreciate an accommodation."

"Fancy that," he said, the grin still in place. "And what might that be?"

"Melvin Jackson."

The grin dimmed.

"Melvin Jackson. Sad story. Nice boy A little misdirected at times, but a nice boy. What's your interest?"

"The father's not pleased his son is being ignored. He asked me to look into it."

"I can see where that might disturb Joshua. What you got?"

"A tie to an old friend of yours. Melvin was indiscreet enough to be seeing the Judge's daughter."

"Yeah, I'd heard that." Birdlegs licked his lips and finished his drink. "Sort of a trip down memory lane, ain't it? Me, the Judge, those holes in you still fresh and all. You gonna be up to it?"

"I finish what I start."

"Even if you need a little help, like those two hoods." He poured for both of us. "Let's cut the shit. It might not have been known to one and all, but those two corpses worked for the Judge. The reason you didn't get dead in the hospital was the Judge put the word out he wanted to put the gun in your mouth himself. He wants you healthy for your death."

"Thoughtful of him. He must be real happy with you, too."

"Not too, but he don't blame me for his daughter's mother being dead."

"She's not dead."

"Might as well be. Can't walk. The way I hear it she can't do nothing a man needs. Makes her dead."

"He shouldn't have sent a woman out to do his dirty work," I said.

"He sent her out because he wanted her dead. Rumors said she'd been getting a real good look at that tattoo of yours. That was why he sent her out. I heard you didn't see it coming."

"Give me the name of your source. He knows more about what I'm thinking than I do."

"That ain't a yes or a no."

"What time of day did that incident with the Judge's wife happen?"

"Don't recall. Daylight. I remember that much."

"When was the last time you saw me in daylight?"

Birdlegs let the grin go wide. "Not since you got done bleeding, but that still ain't no yes or no. Inventive, though. I'm still thinking about that accommodation."

I let out a deep breath. "I didn't see it coming."

"You see the pictures of the not so happy couple in the paper ever so often. The Judge pushing Hildy in her wheelchair, the noble husband standing at her crippled side. Ever notice how she always look like shit, but he's pushing her out there anyway? Not easy looking like shit, a beautiful woman like that. You see those pictures?"

I'd seen them.

"I don't need your help, Birdlegs. I don't need anything from you. Maybe I would if you'd stop lying, but you like a good lie better than most."

"I'm offended."

"Bullshit. Yeah, let's start a new tab, but let's do it minus the myth. Those two guys didn't work for the Judge, and the Judge didn't give a shit if Hildy and I were making it, which is not saying we did. Those two guys were here to shake you down. Must have really pissed you off, the shaker getting shaked. Nice of me to come through the door to save your ass."

"What makes you clairvoyant?"

"My place is down there with the people who make you guys rich. Neither of you have stuck your toe in the real world for so long you've lost touch."

"You might call me and the Judge pillars of the community. Without us it all goes to Hell." He looked at me with the smile gone and with what I thought might be his thoughtful gaze. "Okay, Ace. Forget the accommodation."

I held his eyes and stood.

"Not so fast," Birdlegs said. "Better than an accommodation. A job."

"Got one."

"Okay, same job. Now it pays better. Notice how business is kind of slow out front tonight?"

"I haven't been here in a while."

"It's slow. People staying home. There's a war coming and nobody wants to stumble into the crossfire."

"Melvin and Christina."

"Yeah. Something had to strike the match." He drummed his fingers on his desk. "You gonna blame anyone, blame the Japs for losing the war.   They lose and the shipyard jobs disappear, but damn few folks left town.   White guys came back from the war and wanted jobs so us colored folk wind up sitting on the curb when we ain't standing in the unemployment line."

"You made inroads."

"Some. White guys think shoveling shit is beneath them so we got all the garbage runs and street cleaning jobs. We bid jobs to the city cheaper than what the Judge's white unions were willing to rake off. The city charter say it got to take the lowest bid from an officially sanctioned union and we be sanctioned. Then the Judge's unions sued saying our sanction weren't right, and my, oh my, guess who hear the case? We ain't officially sanctioned no more. Few of my friends got angry and some white unionists fell into the shit fields out west of here. You'll smell them come summer."

"How's that get to war? Sounds more like business as usual."

"We lost a few friends in the scuffle. Take the job and maybe you find out."

"Tell me about Melvin."

"Melvin came by a few times to chat. He sees me as a man of the 'black community.' He says that's how we should call ourselves, not coloreds or Negroes, but blacks. I tell him there ain't nothing in a name. He says he's spending his time studyin' Mr. White and he's learning plenty. Learning how to beat that old Mr. White at his own game."

"What did he mean?" I asked.

Birdlegs shook his head again. "No idea, Ace. But later -- maybe two, three weeks ago -- I hear he comes in on a Wednesday night with some white chick. Didn't know it was the Judge's little girl. Woulda had their picture taken for old times' sake, had I known."

"Yeah, and get them both killed."

"Didn't take no picture and Melvin still dead. I got nothing against the girl, but I pretty damn sure she weren't worth dyin' for."

"Did you see them?"

"Nah, I was . . . tied up." He winked. "There's a light under the bar. It goes on, means I out no matter who shows."

"So, like you said, you ain't got much."

"Not right now but I got eyes all over town. I'll get the word out."

"I wouldn't exactly call us friends," I said, "so how come you're willing to put some of those hard earned bucks in my pocket?"

The big grin came back.

"I trust you. You the man in the middle. Call me tomorrow night 'bout this time. See what I got then."

I stood to leave.

"One more thing, Ace," Birdlegs said. "You ain't by any chance seen Arnold Newman around, have you?"

"Didn't know you two were chums," I said.

"We ain't, but I was just curious if you'd sorta bumped into him."

"If I see him, I'll tell him you asked," I said.

"You see him, it make you the first." He laughed, then pointed at that spot on the floor where two men died. "When those medics came they had two dead and you lying there looking real bad. They put a finger on your neck, and said you was dead, too."

His words poked that ghost of a memory.

"You ever use honeysuckle?" Birdlegs asked.

"Perfume?"

"I don't care where the smell comes from. Just honeysuckle."

"More of a musk man myself. Why?"

"I smelled it when you was lying over there good as dead. But here you are. A miracle. You explain that to me some day."

* * * * *

Downtown Island City shared the same rich tradition for names as the rest of the flood plain. The numbered streets started with First and ended with Ninth, while the lettered streets ran 'A' through 'J.' With one exception. Between Fifth and Sixth ran East Park and West Park, so named for a grassy strip with picnic tables and benches between the two streets. The park blocks, of which there were three stacked one atop the other with their green grass and picnic tables, were the only non-revenue producing blocks in all of downtown. Nobody knew how they got there, but the prevailing wisdom said a wealthy wife wanted a picnic spot when she went shopping.

North of the park, revenue kicked in again with bars, SROs – including mine – and retail stores. Because bars made the real money they always occupied the second floor, just above the water line. Most had big windows for customers to use and oversized iron rings sunk in the outside walls to tie up the boats in the bad floods. Come Hell or high water, a man's got to have a drink.

Two blocks north of the park, a neon light blinked the name "Frills" in red surrounded by white scallops that suggested lace. The bar sat above a hardware store. The stairs only had lights toward the bottom. By the time you reached the bar's doorway your eyes had already adjusted to the smoky dimness waiting inside. When I entered, about half the tables scattered strategically around the room had patrons. Most were occupied by one man, and you could have dropped a bomb on their heads without them noticing.

Men went to Frills to catch a glimpse of what they weren't supposed to see. For a few bucks they could get a real good look. On what used to be the dance floor, six small cocktail tables sat in a half circle. At each table sat a woman with her legs crossed. If you wanted a better look you went to her table and gave her some money. The amount mattered. Once the deal closed and the guy went back to his table, the dame signaled the bartender and a spot light came on that aimed up her skirt. The light would stay on for five minutes. Well-turned calves and flaring thighs caught the eye, but the real stars were extra-long garter belts that showed a lot of skin between the tops of the nylon stocking and the side panel of frilly panties. There was a lot of leg crossing and squirming. How much depended on the customer's deposit.

I walked to a spot where the babe farthest from the door could see me.   Her light was off.

"Hey, Maxine."

"Ace! Got a special new move. For you it's a real good look for only ten bucks."

Her deep, throaty voice added spice to her pin-up girl appearance.

"Max, no offense, but you ain't got much I haven't seen."

"You got a photographic memory?"

"Just want to sit and share some words. Might be more money in small talk. Money you don't have to pay the house."

"A girl has her needs. Sit down. I get a customer you may have to move aside."

"Give him to one of the others."

"Can't. I'm getting a reputation. I wasn't kidding about that new move."

"What is it?"

"Five bucks just to hear me tell you. It'll give you something to think about when you're in bed alone tonight."

I peeled a five off a small roll.

"I hooked a garter into the outside edge of the crotch of my new pink knickers. The elastic runs across my stomach and up my arm to a sleeve band. I spread that arm and it pulls the edge of the panties toward the middle. It works great. One guy damned near fainted."

"Makes you a regular tease."

"I'm just like everything else in this town. What you see is *not* what you get."

"That's it for five bucks?"

"You want to hear where that elastic band rubs? Oh, I had to shave. The garter kept pulling hair. Hurt like a son of a bitch."

"Use the five for a down payment on what I want to talk to you about."

"Quiet! I got me a live one headed this way. Honey," she asked the guy, "how much you want to see?"

"I hear you got something worth showing."

"The new move with all the frills? Twenty bucks." The guy hesitated. "Nobody gets to see but you." He still dangled. "They're pink tonight. Lace in the right place at the top of the best set of legs since Betty Grable."

A twenty hit the table.

"Sit right over there, honey."

She waited until the guy got seated and then repositioned her chair to give him the best view. She signaled to the bartender and her floor light came on.

"Twenty bucks is a little steep," I said. "That feeds a family of five for a week."

"Sort of sets the priorities, doesn't it? What do you want?"

"What's new with the Judge?"

She laughed and I saw a knee clear the table top as she crossed her legs in the other direction.

"I'll have to check with my secretary, but I think he's a little late getting his schedule in. Why you asking me about the Judge?"

"You got the best set of ears in this part of town."

"Among several other nice sets."

"Max, I'm trying to talk here."

"And I'm working! You don't want to hear about boobs and curly short hairs – if I still had any – catch me somewhere else. Hey, hey, watch his face. Here comes the move."

She slowly stretched her arm toward me as the knee came into view. I saw the guy's mouth come open. Next his tongue licked his lips. Max began slowly waving her arm.

"What are you doing?"

"Now you see it, now you don't. Hope he's got a hanky."

"Okay, that's it. How about the Virginia Café later?"

"I'll be there at ten past. Order me a steak san. Tell them it's for Rosie."

The light went off and she swiveled in her chair to put her legs under the table. I stood up and tipped my hat. The customer came back and dropped another twenty on the table.

"Sorry, Sweetie. You gotta have a note from your doctor saying your heart can take it. Had a guy keel over during an encore. Heart quit." She snatched the twenty and stuck it in her cleavage. "Just kidding. Get nice and comfy."

I headed for the stairs and didn't look back.

I must have got turned around coming out of Frills, but that didn't explain why the Virginia Café was on the wrong side of the street. It sat two blocks over from my flop. I'd walked there dozens of times. I stood looking at the street that seemed familiar in every way, but buildings were slightly different, like there'd been a makeover while I was gone. I shook it off, and entered the front door.

The Virginia Cafe hadn't been closed since the last big flood. The owner had ten kids, all of whom could fill a sandbag faster than a longshoreman, and he stayed open as long as he could hold the water out of the kitchen. It was no big deal if the water leaked in around the tables, because if the water was that high everybody wore waders anyway. Another sure sign of spring were the shovels by the door at the Virginia.

I ate there enough for them to know if it was before three in the morning I wanted dinner. After three meant breakfast. Because the blue plate special didn't change until six a.m., it was still Tuesday's meat loaf.

"One on the way, Ace," called Morris, the night cook, through his peep hole from the kitchen.

"Add a steak san for Rosie. Okay?"

The Virginia was a high-class joint. The red vinyl-topped counter stools turned without screeching and none of them had slits leaking stuffing, or were patched with gray tape. Ten booths sat under the windows, and five more lined the wall furthest from the door. A booth held two diners comfortably but not four. I sat away from the windows. Reba, the night girl, came in from the back and waved the coffee pot at me. I nodded.

Half way through the cup, a woman came in the front door. She wore a bandana over her hair, a polka dot blouse buttoned sedately one down from the top, and baggy-brown trousers that touched her shoes. She wore no makeup, and wire-rimmed glasses sat on her nose. She headed for my booth.

"On the way, Rosie," Morris called, and Reba reached for another mug.

Maxine had changed into Rosie the Riveter. She wasn't old enough to have worked in a defense plant, but she had the mid-war look down cold.

"Nice," I said.

"How'd you know it was me?"

"No matter who you pretend to be, you walk like you. I like your walk even if you're not showing any skin."

"I don't show nothing for free."

"Who else you got in your repertoire?"

"Who do you need?"

"The Shadow, maybe. The clock ticking?"

She nodded and pushed the glasses up her nose.

"Either the Judge or Birdlegs are gearing up for a shooting war, or there's a joker in the deck. I need to know which."

"I'm flattered. Big job. You paying or passing it on?"

"Passing it on." Between Jackson and Birdlegs the pockets ran deep.

"What's the budget?" she asked.

"Enough."

"The joker – if there is one – got a name?"

"Arnold Newman's name came up."

"The boogeyman." She wiggled her fingers and made a face you'd use to scare a kid. "He's handy. You want to drop some blame or duck a wrap, blame Arnold. It's like a get-out-of-jail-free card. Anyone actually ever see this guy?"

"Birdlegs expected me to say I had, but I haven't. In my cop days, I wondered if it was an alias. Now, I think there's something out there, and it ain't the Judge or Birdlegs."

"Why?"

"Let's say our local pair of kings shoot it out and one wins. What's the Judge going to do with Birdlegs's empire? Run it himself? No way. Same's true for Birdlegs. The white thugs going to let him run things? No. Those guys been talking about doing each other in for five years, but they're still splitting the take."

"You share this theory with anyone else?" Max asked.

"Nobody wants to hear it. Island City is fantasyland. Things are divvied up, the cops know who the bad guys are, and the honest Joes stay out of the way." I pointed at the shovel by the Virginia's door. "Unless Mario starts filling sandbags, it's copasetic."

"Leaving the unknown Arnold Newman to trump both kings. Nice idea, but Arnold has the same problem as our kings, only times two. Who's going to listen?"

"That's a clue. He's someone with a plan that includes that particular solution. Max, I need results."

"I'll start poking around."

I leaned back and admired her Rosie the Riveter persona as our dinners hit the table.

"When you're wearing one of your disguises, I've probably walked by you on the street and didn't see you." She smiled and winked. "You should have gone to Hollywood."

She shook her head, but the smile was gone.

"Three strikes before I get on the show biz train, Ace." She pointed at her glasses. "Blind as a bat without them."

"That's one."

"My voice sounds like a gravel truck going uphill."

"Does not. Besides, I like it."

"Wanna make a movie? Strike three is I can't act."

"You do a helluva job at Frills."

"I'm not acting. I'm just showing off. I love it. I started giving glimpses of my undies when I was eight to get a seat on the streetcar. Blending in on the street is the opposite of acting. I never want to get noticed."

I cut off a bite of meat loaf and painted on a layer of mashed.

"Here's my thinking on your assignment," I said. "If a white guy could find the answer it would have been found. So how about black guys? Birdlegs has his unseen eyes all over town, but here he is asking me to look, meaning black don't work either. I need fresh eyes, Max. A woman's touch. I think there's a new paradigm, but I'm not seeing it."

"Nice word."

"I'm educated. So are you. In fact, we have a lot in common."

"You trying to wiggle in close?"

"No. I want you to keep your eye on the ball. It's dangerous out there."

"But not so dangerous you're afraid to send me out."

"You and me, we got pushable START buttons. Woozy winds me up and nothing keeps me out of the game. I pressed yours. You crack the Newman puzzle and you'll have clients who don't care about your undies."

"If I'm that good, maybe I could make more on my own."

"How much is it worth having me covering your back?"

She chewed a big bite of sandwich. When her mouth was empty she held up her coffee cup.

"As long as I've known you, you've always been a regular Sir Galahad. Okay. Business partners, but what's this me and you thing? You just like getting laid every so often, or is there more to us?"

"Is there more to it for you?"

"I asked first. I get enough tire kickers at Frills."

I stared at her and had another of those déjà vu moments that were coming too often now to ignore. They came with a slight blurring of my vision. The blurring bothered me the most. I had to have good eyesight in this job or I wasn't going to last. I shook off the feeling and focused on Max.

"For me, Max, you remind me how good it is to be alive."

"Who else you got reminding you? Not that I'm the jealous type."

I smiled and showed her my empty hand.

"Wow. An exclusive," Maxine said. "You don't gotta."

"Yeah, I do. It makes it simpler. Before I died, I took a lot for granted. Now I don't."

Another blurring. This time it was the words and the feeling as I said them. I'd been here before.

"Honey," she said in the tone that turned up the heat, "you need a booster shot of the good life, you give me a call."

We ate and I thought about her. When she finished she pushed her plate back.

"One thing, Galahad. If I'm working, don't get too close. You don't blend in as well as I do. Better yet. When I'm working, don't cover my back at all. I'll be in touch when I have something for you."

Chapter 4

I got lucky working on Joshua Jackson's list of Melvin's friends. I found Vincent Williams and Jerome Pitney at Bork's Rib Pit on D Street. I'd missed Williams at the laundry where he worked, but they told me he usually ate at Bork's. Pitney was a bonus.

The roasting pits built into the brick wall filled the inside with aromatic smoke from the slow-cooking beef or pork ribs, chicken or hot links. I ordered pork with the hot sauce and corn on the cob. It came with a slice of white bread on a paper plate. A draft beer made it a complete meal. Williams and Pitney sat at a table covered with a red and white checked oil cloth. The only other customers were two old men at the counter who swiveled their stools to face each other while they rolled dice out of a leather cup, slamming it on the bar and slowly lifting the edge to eye their count. Their lips moved as they talked to the die. Sarah Vaughan sang "Embraceable You" on the Wurlitzer in the corner.

I'd introduced myself to Williams and Pitney when I came in and told them what I wanted. They had a chance to think about it while I ordered at the counter. Vincent Williams made a phone call, but beat me back to the table.

"Mizz Jackson say you tellin' the truth, so what you want?" Vincent asked while he worked at spotting the next bite on his rib.

"Reasons. Whoever killed Melvin had them. Where was he working?"

Jerome Pitney hadn't said a thing, but held up his hand before Vincent answered.

"What's it worth to you?" Jerome asked, pushing the hand toward me.

"Joshua said you were his son's friends. I pay you for what you ought to be happy to give, and bill Joshua. You feel like hitting him up for money right now?"

"Shit. He got it, I don't," said Jerome. "Some think he's hot shit – not everybody." He licked sauce off his fingers. "Ain't worth nothing, nothing is what you get."

"No sir, Jerome," Vincent said. "We gonna talk to this man. Melvin, he meant something to me. We both know he was asking for trouble. We warned him."

"You're a fool, Vince," Jerome said. "White man just wants to know what you know. Maybe you're asking for trouble just like Melvin."

"No, I don't think so," Vincent said. "His momma say help, I help."

The rib Jerome had been gnawing fell from his fingers and he pushed his chair back.

"This man here, he got his own way of finding what he need. He don't need your smart mouth making things easy for him. When the last time anybody make it easy for you?"

Vincent Williams wore a gray slouch hat pulled down on his forehead. He pushed it back and stared at me.

"You think this man got it easy?" he asked more to himself than to either Pitney or me. "No, I don't rightly believe that. Not if he gonna find who killed Melvin. Melvin wasn't stupid. He had dreams. Big dreams. He knew he was stepping outside seeing that white girl and talking over his station. Maybe he was asking for it, but he was sly, and finding who done it ain't gonna be easy."

"Vince, goddamn it!" Pitney stood while Vincent talked, then leaned forward with both fists on the table. "Keep it up and see what happens."

Williams watched as his friend left, letting the screen door on a spring slam behind him. The argument hadn't bothered the dice game at the counter. That was one thing about being low on the ladder. The only trouble worth noticing was your own.

"It wasn't easy being Melvin's friend," Vince said. "I don't think he knew he was different than the rest of us cuz he had money. He never thought about things like why he had better clothes, or a full stomach, or why the rest of us settled for what he called trash jobs."

He sighed and finished his beer. I'd eaten a few bites, and the hot sauce burned my lips.

"Melvin was busin' at the Island City Athletic Club," he said. "He'd been there maybe a month, maybe a little longer."

"Busing tables?" I asked. "Sounds like a trash job."

"I asked him what he was doing in a place like that, but he just grinned and said he had a plan."

"He say what?"

"Just that he had a plan," Vincent repeated. He picked up his empty beer mug and started to stand.

"On me," I said. He shook his head.

"I'm buying this one for Melvin," he said, and headed for the counter.

"One more thing," I said, and he stopped. "Christina Bell. Did he talk about her?"

Williams tapped the empty mug against the palm of his hand.

"Funny about that. He never said nothing, but she was part of the plan."

"How do you know?"

"I saw them together a couple of times. They didn't look all lovey-dovey. They looked more like they was on a job together. If she was part of his plan then it was her plan, too."

He bought a draft and tossed it down in one long pull. He nodded at me as he left. The door closed quietly.

If Melvin was "studying Mr. White" like he'd told Birdlegs, he'd picked the right place. The Island City A.C. membership made up the local Who's Who. Only the right white men became full members. Women and children of these right men held family memberships and could swim and eat and mix with their own, but had no say in how the club was run.

At the A.C. the downstairs game room was the heart of Island City. Only two types regularly made it inside – members and menials. I'd bullied my way in a couple of times when I still carried a badge. The movers and shakers barely tolerated me, but the menials came and went like wraiths. If that was the only place the answer to Melvin's plan could be found I was in trouble. Unless I came at it from the other side, the Christina Bell side.

I ate the rest of my ribs and diluted the hot sauce with the beer.

When I left Bork's, two guys leaned on my jalopy. When they saw me, the one in front held up his hands and slowly opened his coat to show he wasn't strapped. I stopped my hand halfway into my jacket then nodded to the second man to show his good faith, too. He did, but his eyes never left where my hand dipped into my coat.

"You know who we are, Spader?" the one in front asked.

"How's the Judge?"

"He wants to see you."

"Where, and don't me tell me up at his place?"

"He figured you'd say that. May I put my hand in my coat? It's just paper."

"Slow, and fingers only."

The hand played square. The minion waved the note at me. I pointed at the top of my car.

"It's a phone number. Call him soon, Spader."

Their job done, the two walked into the alley behind Bork's without losing sight of me and my hand. I heard car doors slam, an engine start, and then fade. I picked up the paper. I went into Bork's and dropped a nickel into the pay phone.

"Spader?" the voice asked.

I agreed it was me.

"You know why I'm calling?" it asked.

"I'm curious."

"You know you don't have a friend in this town?"

"No, I didn't know that."

"It's true. The cops hate you because you were a pain in their ass when you worked for them, and since you don't you're a nobody. You and I know how we stand, and Greer may not shoot you but you two will never be friends. That's everybody, but here you are, still the man in the middle."

"Am I supposed to agree?"

"No. Listen close. I had nothing to do with Melvin Jackson's death."

"Gee, nothing but the truth so help you God? Since you didn't do it and his parents want to know who did, where should I look next?"

"I don't care. I've got a job for you."

"I've got a job."

"You will take this one," the Judge said, his voice flat and his diction perfect. "If you don't, you won't earn your other fees."

"If I say no, you going to shoot me again?"

"How about you listen with your brain and turn the mouth off? I want to see you. No risk."

"Where?"

"You pick. I may not agree, but try."

"The Island A.C. In the game rooms. Should work for you. Get a private room and no one has to know you're slumming."

"Why there?"

"I love the potato salad."

After a short wait, he said, "Agreed. Nine p.m. You know the rule."

The rule was you didn't take a weapon inside the A.C. Nobody wanted their kids getting gunned down making the A.C. the safest place in Island City.

"One more question," he said. "You ever think about being rich? Moving to someplace a little nicer?"

"Not before a couple of days ago."

"Think about it again."

Dotty Orland ran the Stanford Clipping Agency out of a third floor office in a building with no elevator. She'd been a nurse turned war reporter, covering the march toward Japan's home island one bloody Pacific atoll at a time. A correspondent died in her arms, but before he did he handed her his notebook and told her to file his story. She had a knack, she'd told me. When she'd reached Island City she stayed in the biz, at least by her definition. I'd used Dotty when I was a cop and paid for her myself. The city wouldn't, because they thought we ought to do our own detecting.

"You're good copy, Spader," she'd laugh right before giving me a break on the price. "Where would I be without people like you?"

I'd never met anyone named Stanford in the office and had asked about the name. She said Stanford sounded smart and Orland didn't.

A bell rang in the back as I opened the door marked PRIVATE. She didn't encourage drop-ins.

"Spader!" Dotty called as she looked up from a big table covered with newspapers. "I heard you were dead!"

Wire-rimmed glasses sat halfway down her nose and scissor handles stuck out of her tight bun of gray hair. Her blue eyes started at my hat, and trailed downward. She walked around the counter and gave me a hug. "Seeing you makes me believe in life after death."

"Jeez, I don't know what to say, Dotty."

"Not sharing the secret? Give me a clue. Should I go to church more?"

"Up to you. I don't. Christina Bell. You got anything?"

"A herniated disc from lifting her file."

She walked into the stacks. Five-drawer filing cabinets sat in rows that disappeared into the gloom of the large office. She stopped at one and pulled out a thick manila envelope, then went deeper into the cavernous recesses of the stacks.

I lost sight of her until she came back with a second thick folder. She dropped them on the counter.

I read CHR BELL printed in heavy black ink on both.

"You know my filing system. Crime, commerce, society, and gossip. These are her society and gossip clips. I'm thinking I should open a crime file. What do you think?"

I opened the society envelope. Most of the clippings showed Christina at dances at the A. C. and other ballrooms I didn't recognize. The daughter had Hildy's blond hair and dramatic features and her father's sturdy physique, a combination guaranteed to turn heads. In most of the photos she stood with other young women who no doubt knew no one looked at them after they saw Christina.

"Spader? You got wax in your ears? Should I start the other file?"

"Yeah, and keep it handy." I pointed at the others. "You got anything with her and Melvin Jackson?"

"Yeah. One. It's in his file. I got it under the table."

Under the table meant if I wanted to take a look it would cost me.

"Let's see."

She came back with a thin envelope and pulled out a glossy.

Island City would not be happy with the portrayed exercise in racial tolerance. The beautiful Christina stood with an arm draped over the shoulders of the handsome Melvin. The black and white photo captured the moment. She wore a low-necked top that showed off her cleavage and Melvin wore a suit with his white shirt opened an extra button. His serious look contrasted with her challenging smile.

"That the Lullaby?"

"Yep. Those two were asking for it."

I turned the photo over.

"Who's William I. Travis?"

"He was one of the hyenas that followed Christina around. Most of his stuff is crap. He took pictures of her everywhere. The girl didn't have much in the way of privacy."

Her phone rang. While she answered I pored over the rest of Christina's file. Dotty's shrill voice came through loud and clear.

"Hon, you're too late! I've got that. Anything else?" Dotty raised her voice. "You know my rates. I pay five bucks for gossip if it's fresh." She listened. "I'm interested and yes, I'd pay more. Wait a second." She waved at me and pointed at the phone. "She says she has something on Christina. You interested?"

"Who is she?"

"Delinda Paz." She waved a hand at the photos on the table. "The dance at the A.C. She's the one in the back."

"Yeah. Get an address. I pay better than you do."

"Will you sell to me if it's any good?"

"If you want it, it's yours. Free."

Dotty got the info and hung up. I copied the name and number of the photographer off the back of the glossy and then held up another ballroom shot.

"Where and when was this one taken?"

"The Silver Lining Ballroom at Sunnyvale Beach. The hall's pretty new, so probably taken last summer. Why you asking?"

"That's mother and daughter in one frame. That didn't like each other. Wonder why they're together in this one."

Last summer Christina was supposed to be lying low suffering from remorse. And her mother was standing – no wheelchair. I stared at the photo. The picture should be a couple of years older than the date.

The Island City Athletic Club took up five blocks against the southern flank of the Calder Hills. In the next big flood, when the rest of the lowlands slid beneath the waves, the A.C. would do no worse than get its skirt wet.

It needed five square blocks because the greyhound track in their backyard took up three of them. The balcony looked down on the puppies as they chased the mechanical rabbit around and around, and had an electronic hook up with the pari-mutuel windows where the riff-raff wagered.

My car didn't do so well up-hill, so I'd taken the streetcar. The livery for the help at the A.C. consisted of tasteful black waist coats, starched white shirts, red bow ties, and creased gray slacks atop black, highly shined shoes. Most who wore the get-up were black and had stony game faces firmly in place. I saw two who spotted me. I figured Birdlegs would know about my visit during their next break.

The afternoon messenger from the Judge waited outside the door.

"Where's your uniform?" I asked. He stared at me. "If looks could kill, huh?"

"You'd be dead," he said, face and voice devoid of emotion.

I followed him to the elevator. When the door opened he went in first. The Negro elevator man wrinkled his nose as he saw me. I wondered which of the help would win the race to Birdlegs with news of my incursion into enemy territory.

"You're pushing your luck, Spader," the messenger said, as the car squeaked down. "If the Judge didn't want you safe and sound for this little job, you'd have never made it this far."

He knew his every word would be repeated back to the Spew sending a lot of questions my way. I waited in silence and followed him out of the car. I winked at the elevator man.

The elevator opened on to a hallway. First door on the right led into the billiards room. Four gleaming wood tables with their immaculate green fields of felt sparkled under hanging lamps with Tiffany shades. Three were billiards and the fourth was snooker. The snooker table had three players all dressed in formal wear. They were serious shooters. Their coats had deep vents to free their shoulders for the long reaches across the large table. I guessed it was a money game since they were playing with a full rack of red balls that would stretch the game and build the score.

Next door was the card room. The money games at the A.C. were bridge at two cents a point and no limit stud poker. The room was full and the air hung heavy with cigar smoke. Again men wore formal wear. I didn't see anyone minus a tie. A bar with two bartenders shared the card room wall with the billiards room so drinks could be served to both rooms out of the same bar.

Smaller rooms came next. Rooms where the games were more intimate and the stakes higher. Not all the games required cards. On two of the knobs hung signs that announced they were in use. The second one with a sign got knocked on, and then was opened. The messenger held it for me as I went in. The hatred poured off his face.

"See you," I said. I heard the door close, and said to the Judge, "He doesn't like me."

"No one does."

"Not true, but very few people who like you like me."

"Potato salad and scotch on the bar. Ring the bell if you want anything else."

I hadn't been kidding about the potato salad and dished myself a plate. It was the one thing I remembered fondly from previous, official visits. The label on the bottle said the single malt scotch was older than me. I poured an appreciative glass straight up.

The Judge sat at a poker table that held neither cards nor chips. The color in his highball glass said the scotch was neat and that the Judge could still belt it away. I toasted the Judge with the glass and the salad.

"You are currently being paid," the Judge began, "by Joshua Jackson to find out who killed his son. Greer is paying you more to do the same thing and while you're at it, find out if Arnold Newman is back in town."

"What color's my underwear? You know everything else."

"Leave the jokes at the door. I am in no mood. My daughter's missing."

I set my glass down in a holder in the empty chip tray and pulled a side table over for the salad.

"How long?"

"About the same time the Jackson boy was killed."

"No word?"

"Nothing." He looked at me. "Spader. I mean literally nothing."

"As if she'd never existed?" I asked, remembering Woozy's words about Melvin's disappearance.

The effort to hide his feelings took its toll on Judge Ulysses Bell. His face softened around the eyes and the mouth. A glistening of the eyes vouched for the truth of his words.

"I want you to find her," he said. "The assignment is not in conflict with your other tasks and pays the best of all for results. I want her back and alive. If the latter is beyond your power I want names and silence. Clear?"

"Does Hildy know?"

I watched his face as I asked the question. It stayed neutral but some of its usual hardness returned.

"Of course. She's the girl's mother." He took a long pull from the glass, emptied it, and walked to the bar to reload. "Lock the door."

I did, although I couldn't imagine anyone walking in on him.

"You know I didn't order you killed," he said.

"No, I don't know that, although I suspect you're telling the truth. If you did, it wasn't about Hildy, though."

"You dead would have been inconvenient."

"Yeah, hard to find somebody to confide in. Risky, too, if you're wrong."

"You're the only man in town who knows the score. You know more than either Greer or I. If I had to say anyone was Arnold Newman I'd say it was you."

"Why would I do that?"

"Indeed, and that is the problem. You have never shown one ounce of entrepreneurial inclination. Greer's and my animosity keeps you gainfully employed."

"You keep fanning the flames with Greer. He says you're getting greedy."

"There has to be give and take." He sipped his drink. "Greer and I -- we are the 'us' and 'them.' I get ahead, he gets even. I made some gains with the union ruling I sent down. I cheated. Greer's already appealing it to another court where it will be reversed and we're back to normal. Then he'll have the edge with his black unions and catch up his losses."

I sipped my glass and ate some salad while I thought about what he'd said.

"Birdlegs wants to know what's really happening."

"So do I," the Judge shot back. "He suggested Arnold Newman?"

"Yes."

"Has he met with Newman?"

"He says no and I believe him. I heard Newman called a bogey-man. A sort of Mr. Nobody. Something goes wrong and he gets the blame."

"You don't think he exists?"

"Seeing is believing. I haven't seen him and I doubt you have either. But that aside, you didn't kill Melvin Jackson. Christina would have figured you for it and made your life hell. Birdlegs didn't take her. There was nothing but grief in it for him. He's just using Melvin and your ruling to stir my blood so I'll look for Newman. That means someone else is in town. Maybe it's Arnold Newman. Maybe a different Mr. Nobody."

"And here's to Dan T," the Judge said, raising his glass. "The man in the middle taking money from all sides."

"Not all sides. Only the side of the angels. How come it took three days to call off the hounds on the Jackson murder?"

"Why would I call it off? When I found out Christina was missing, the police were looking for who killed the boy. That meant they might find her in their efforts. When they stopped, I figured they took heat about a race case and decided to cut their losses."

"If the cops didn't shut it down, and my inside friends say they didn't, we're back to Mr. Nobody. That's the good news. Means I'm looking for something that's there."

"What's next?"

"Christina. You sure she didn't take off on her own?"

"No."

"Then I have to talk to Hildy."

"Why?"

"She's the girl's mother." I paused. "Of course."

He glared at me, but the job he'd assigned me held him in check.

"Do it when I'm not around. You probably remember where the back door is."

I ignored the jab.

"She always in the wheelchair?"

"I don't know. We don't see each other. She stay's upstairs. I'm down."

"Up? What about the stairs?"

"There's an elevator." He put his glass down and held me with his hard-ass stare. "What I said about replacing you being an inconvenience. I've been inconvenienced before."

Chapter 5

I left the Island A.C. shortly after midnight. The streetcars only ran twice an hour so, I walked. I turned my collar up against the mild rain, and shared the sidewalks with others who got off their jobs too late for rides. We all headed downhill to where the real people lived. Most of us fetched drinks, food, sex, and in my case information, for those who had more than we did.

I stopped at a booth and called Hildy. It was a number I remembered well. She'd always been a late night person. A maid answered and said Miss Hildegard had retired. I told her who I was and made an appointment for the next night at ten. Apparently the maid had the authority. I hung up and kept walking.

The Judge and Birdlegs had both called me the man in the middle, implying that I took orders from everyone. My role was like a referee to keep both sides talking and not shooting, and make good money along the way. If there was a third player in town the shooting would start, and those of us on the sidewalk would be the first ones hit. Make that third player the fourth. The cops already had third place for themselves, although they weren't serious players. Yet.

I wanted to find Woozy, and since Woo Fong Louie's was his favorite place to eat at the end of his shift, I headed for Chinatown. The rain let up and I kept walking rather than catch the car when it clattered by. It was full and I didn't feel like riding on the running board.

Louie had more cops on the cuff than the city payroll including some ex-cops. I ate free because I'd done him a service. His youngest daughter, Flower -- she'd called herself Cheryl at the time -- had run away and he wanted her back. When I hauled her home after rejecting her offers of heavenly bliss, he told me I'd dine on his gratitude for eternity.

"You are a foolish man," Flower said, pulling away from her father and rubbing her hand over my stomach, "putting this ahead of other hungers." She'd laughed at me, then at her father. I turned to him, bowed, and told him I would be honored to receive his gratitude. He studied my face and returned the bow. We both knew his troubles were a long way from over. Now I never ordered, just ate the delicacies they placed before me.

Flower saw me when I came in and rubbed her stomach with a big smile then disappeared as Louie waved to me. We talked before he took me to Woozy and Pugh. They sat in their usual booth near the back. Woozy ate chow mein and Chinese snow peas with beef, while Pugh slurped at a giant bowl of woo suey gao.

"Suppose you want your old seat, Ace," Pugh said, with a laugh, and slapping the six inches of unused bench space at his side.

Pugh's laugh sounded like a pipe organ breathing a full bellows at the low end of the scale. His head showed where the rim of his hat hugged his scalp. His hairline was in full retreat, but his moustache and goatee were thick and luxurious and free of any gray. He and Woozy made a pair. When they got in a car you could hear the springs settling somewhere near the rims. Their combined weight was over a quarter ton and divided equally, although Woozy stood six inches taller.

"Nah, stay where you are," I said. "I'll rough it out here on the end."

I pulled a chair over.

"Can always tell how the economy's doing," Woozy said forking in his peas and beef. "More peas than meat means things ain't bad."

Pugh and I had heard his wisdom often enough to know it didn't need an answer.

Lin, one of Flower's older sisters, brought tea and poured.

"Ever notice, Jesse," Woozy said around a fingernail as he picked at a piece of beef stuck in his teeth, "how service gets better when Ace comes in."

Pugh pushed back his bowl and lifted his beltline off the table so it could settle lower.

"Long as he sits with us," he said, taking a toothpick from his shirt pocket and probing a molar. Compared to Wozinsky, it was a delicate operation. "Talk to Jackson?"

I nodded. "And Birdlegs."

"What Birdlegs have to say?" Pugh asked.

"Says to hunker down. War's coming."

Woozy pushed the last of the chow mein around his plate, and belched. He pointed at me with his chopsticks.

"Yeah, we heard that one. He say who gonna shoot whom?"

"Who do you think?" I asked Woozy.

Lin brought my dinner and placed it before me with both hands.

"What the hell's that?" Pugh asked.

"Cashew lobster with lychee nuts, and shrimp fried rice," she said.

"Lobster?" Pugh asked.

"Yeah, lobster," I said. "Big claws and antennae waving out of their heads."

"I know what the fuck lobster is," Pugh answered. "I just never ate any."

"Lin, how about doing the honors family style?" I asked.

She bowed her head and deftly split the portions in thirds, serving each of us. Pugh lifted his belt with one hand and picked up his fork with the other.

"Lobster?" he said again, taking a piece, and placing it in his mouth. He chewed slowly and rolled it around his mouth. "Lobster. You ain't seen the Judge?"

"I've only been working this a day or so," I said.

Woozy finished his portion and reached for mine. I slapped his hand. "I came to ask questions not to share my dinner."

"Ask fast," Woozy muttered around a stolen mouthful.

"You guys sure this is a pissing match between the Judge and Birdlegs's?"

"The timing bothers me," Pugh said, and dropped his fork on the plate. "Three days to call us off. Either we get the case or we don't. That's the way it always goes. How come we already sweating when they send us to the bench?"

"Ace's question means," Woozy said, the chopsticks now pointed at Pugh, "is there someone horning in on the Judge?"

"Horning in?"

"Yeah. If he didn't do what he usually does, yet it happened, who did it? The Judge don't like anybody playing his hand. Right, Ace?"

"Couldn't have said it that way myself, Woozy."

"'S'cuse me," Pugh said, rapping his empty bowl with his fork, "but you two geniuses are saying that old fart didn't have nothing to do with whatever it is we're talking about? As far as I know you ain't even asked him."

"I can tell you this," Woozy said. "Word has it the Judge was out of town for those three days. He gets back and the case gets pulled."

"That seals it for me," Pugh said. "Timing adds up."

Woozy shook his head.

"Those three days was the reason I gave Ace's name to Jackson. This ain't business as usual."

"I still don't get it," Pugh said.

"I heard Christina Bell is missing," I said.

"Shit!" Woozy said. "Didn't hear that."

"How come you heard it?" Pugh asked me.

"Because I asked the question. I talked to the Judge on the phone."

"You got his private number?" Woozy asked, giving me a narrow-eyed look.

"I called the number that hard ass who works for him told me to call. The Judge wants me to find his kid."

"Ain't that some kind of conflict of interest?" Pugh asked.

"Depends," I said. "Maybe whoever shot Jackson took the girl. Same case. Maybe the girl got snatched because Jackson got shot. Different folks but one led to the other. Still the same case."

"Yeah, fat pay day, too," Woozy dropped his chopsticks, a sign he was pissed. "You gonna sell Joshua Jackson out?"

"You know me better than that. Jackson comes first, Birdlegs second, and the Judge only if it works for me."

"Or if you gotta see Hildy," Woozy said. "You still got the hots for her?"

I pushed my plate back with food still on it and neither went for it.

"I'm not a cop. I don't have to answer to Captain Yes-sir, or anyone else who is in someone's pocket. I can go where I want and that's what I'm doing. Imagine if you could do that?"

Woozy picked up his sticks while Pugh still chewed on the words.

"What else is going on?" I asked.

"Crimes up," Pugh said.

Woozy and I ignored him. Woozy looked at the ceiling.

"Been thinking about that," Woozy said, pinching a chunk of lobster off my plate. "Seeing some pretty goddamn strange promotions the last few months. Lots of old-timers, and lots of dickheads from the sticks climbing faster than some of us downtown hangers on. They stick together. Sort of reminds me of a clique."

"What kind of clique?" I asked.

"Incompetence is its own reward. If you're a fuck-up who can't find his desk chair, you goin' up, baby."

"How about angels?" I asked. "Whose golden boys are on the rise?"

"Don't know. Can't tie them to any of the usual crowd, and that bothers me. If you know who owns them, you know who to watch your back against. Told Jesse the other night -"

"Last night," Pugh said.

"Last night, it's like the cops got a new owner and they're cleaning house."

"How about Pinella?"

"Captain Yes-sir? King of the fuck-ups? That shit," Pugh said.

"He's in on it, but I don't know any more than I told you yesterday. He's been an incompetent asshole so long he just sorta blends in with the rest of them."

"Why don't you talk to him yourself, Ace," Pugh laughed. "You remember how much he loves you."

"Might do that, Jesse. When all this change start?" I asked Woozy.

"Right after you got shot and lived."

Pugh attacked the dinner Woozy had left on my plate and asked with his mouth full, "You sure the Judge be the one who had you gunned down?"

"Very good question," I said, and pushed the plate closer to him. "What makes you ask?"

"I ain't no Sherlock Holmes, but coincidence bugs me. Like those three days. The Judge comes back and the case closes. Back then you get shot 'cuz you doing the Judge's wife, or so it seems. No reason to ask around 'cuz it's the Judge, then all this weird shit starts."

"You guys ever think I wasn't doing Hildy? That I just wanted everybody to think I was?"

"If you doin' that," Pugh said, "that be the weirdest shit of all."

"But think about this," I said. "If they wanted me dead how come I ain't?"

"They did," Woozy said.

"What?"

"Want you dead. They tried again. Me and Jesse pulled a little extra duty, volunteer type, while you were in the hospital. They tried twice. Then one day you were gone. Moved someplace so mysterious no one knew."

I stared at them.

"Why didn't you tell me?"

"You'd have done the same for either of us, but we had a good reason for saying nothing."

"What?"

"You save someone's life and don't say nothing, it ain't on you to take care of them."

"Yeah," Pugh added. "We save your life and tell you, then we're responsible till the day you do die. We don't want no pain in the ass."

"So you guys saved my life twice," I said, and shook my head. It would take time to integrate this. "Now you admit it means you have to watch out for me?"

Woozy and Pugh exchanged looks.

"Ain't there some kind of statute of limitations on this?" Pugh asked. When Woozy didn't answer, Pugh said, "We got days starting Sunday. You want me watching your back you got to get up earlier."

"There was no reason to tell you," Woozy said. "We don't know who the guys were so what was the point? Besides how we gonna tell you if you ain't around to tell?"

"So why say anything now?"

"It came up. We've wondered about the Judge sending the shooters since the beginning, but we didn't hear no one denying it. We decided to let it sit until the time was right." He spread his hands. "Seems to be now."

Pugh gave a mighty yawn and signaled he was done. We all stood, Pugh left, but Woozy held me back.

"You aren't the only smart guy in town, Ace. I'm ready to listen when you want an ear."

"I don't know, Woozy."

"What don't you know?"

We walked slowly toward the door.

"You ever think this has all happened before?" I asked.

"Over and over. Some days I feel like life is a make-up test. Talk to me when you feel like it."

I looked at him and shook his hand.

I called Birdlegs from a booth outside Louie's.

"Ain't got much yet, Ace, but I'm working on it," he said. "You?"

"Melvin was working the A.C. busing tables. Got anybody there you can tap?"

"Certainly, but you coulda asked around yourself while you were there."

It had been less than two hours since I'd left the Judge.

"I was busy."

"The Judge?"

"Of course. His daughter's missing."

"My, my. And he wants you on the job. That makes, let's see, one, two, and three paychecks. Close to retiring a wealthy man."

"He says you filed an appeal on the union thing and that you'll win. He doesn't see why you got your shorts in a knot."

I waited out a long silence.

"Seems to be a theme here," he finally said. "Perhaps a provocateur sowing seeds of discontent. You ask him about Arnold Newman?"

"Rumors only. He's never seen the guy either."

"For a ghost, that man do get around." More silence. "His daughter. When?"

"Same time as Melvin. The Judge was out of town and didn't know about it."

"Did Hildy know?"

"Haven't asked her."

"But you gonna, right?"

"Tomorrow night at ten. You and the Judge are thinking the same thing. Melvin and Christina about the two best people to lose if you want to start the shooting."

"What do you think?"

"You both talking to me while you get organized. I go out and defuse the situation or get killed. Either way works for you guys."

"Pretty true."

"Who were the guys you shot after they shot me?"

"Yeah." Long silence. "Been wondering that myself. I seen their faces when you came in. They was as surprised at shooting you as you were at getting shot. They were there to threaten me, not to die. Life's a bitch."

"What's that mean? Threatening you?"

"Beats the shit out of me. Saying that a lot these days. You staying on the job?"

"Get me somebody at the A. C. to talk to."

"Yeah. Call me in twenty-four hours. Oh, Ace. Under the circumstances, you working for anybody with a buck, I feel obligated to mention be real bad for your retirement package you lose sight of your priorities. You hear me now?"

"You're hurting my feelings, Birdlegs."

"Hurt more than that if you double cross me."

I hung up. So far I was telling everybody the truth and all they did was threaten me. Seems honesty may not be the best policy.

The streets of Chinatown smelled of tired cooking oil and gleamed from the fresh rain. I felt a hint of spring warmth elbowing at the chill winter air. About time spring showed with Easter two weeks away.

Chapter 6

I slept through the day and awoke damp with perspiration. I fought open the window on the central air shaft. It was the first time it had been open in months. I put my hand out. Definitely warmer even after sunset. I had intended to get up and pay a visit to both the photographer and the woman who'd called Dotty Orland, but it didn't happen. I did call Joshua Jackson and confirm I was on the job. He asked for an update, and I told him I didn't work that way. Things always changed this early in a project and I needed to keep an open mind. He didn't like the idea, but I told him he'd either have to trust me or cut me loose. We hung up and I was still working for him.

I had the blue plate at the Virginia, liver and onions, peas, and mashed potatoes with gravy. I got my car out of the garage, bought a buck's worth of gas and headed for the Calder Hills. My old pre-war auto could manage no grade steeper than about two percent. I took the long way around complete with false starts that left me drifting backwards downhill to try another route. Since my rebirth, I seemed to share basic traits with inanimate objects: the room that never saw the light of day and now a car that only got where it was going by taking the long way around.

The Judge's house, a turn of the century mansion with twenty-four rooms, including eight bedrooms and four baths, sat at the top of the hill, making it the residence with the highest elevation in the city. Hildy's rooms on the top floor gave her a wraparound view. I remembered the view, or at least the lights of the night.

The dashboard clock said ten twenty. Steam seeped out of the engine compartment as my car gasped the last block. The street ended at the Judge's mansion.

It was on fire.

The porch light was on, but it wasn't as bright as the flames breaking through the front windows. I saw a Ford, either green or blue, parked under the Judge's porte-cochere.

I left my car on the curb to stay out of the fire department's way and ran for the house. The front corner burned the most intensely leaving the rest of the front in shadow. Out of the dark ran a figure who threw a fiery bundle. A new burst of flame lit the house. He ran for the car, but stopped when he saw me running at him. I saw someone else in the driver's seat. The runner stopped and pulled a gun out of his coat. He got two rounds off before he jumped on the running board as the car started to move. I got a good look with his face frozen over the top of the car. He was colored. The war had started.

I ran back to my car and pulled my shotgun out of the back. With its long barrels, the street cannon handled hard, but loaded with double-aught buck it could do serious damage.

The fire-bombers' car squealed up on its rims as it took the sharp turn into the street. They had to either go by me, or stop and shoot it out. They chose to speed by. The shooter on the running board aimed over the roof and started firing. I got off both barrels, with the first shredding the driver's side, and the second hitting higher at the shooter. He flew off the car as the dead driver lost control and hit a tree in the parking strip. The impact crumpled the car, lifting the rear end before gravity slammed it back.

I turned away from the wreck and ran for the house dropping the shotgun on the way. The fire worked its way across the front. The door stood open. In the doorway lay an empty wheelchair, the top wheel still spinning.

I ran in. Smoke hung close to the ceiling so I could see. If the Judge was home he'd have to manage on his own. I looked for Hildy and didn't see her. I looked up at the flames beckoning to me from the sides of the huge atrium.

"Trial by fire," I said, and thought of Woozy's words.

I took the stairs three at a time. At the second floor landing smoke filled the hallways left and right. Hildy's rooms had been up there, but with her injury I guessed she'd moved down a floor. In the time I wasted discovering I was wrong, the flames had moved closer to the stairs. I heard no fire sounds, no crackling or roaring, no hissing and sighing as walls and curtains reached the flash point. I still had a couple of minutes before the whole upper part of the house went up.

I grabbed a lung full of air laced with smoke and hit the stairs. My feet wanted nothing to do with the choice. I told them they had to move faster or we'd die. Halfway up I hit the smoke line and my visibility shrank to a stair at a time. I crab-walked to the top floor.

I saw a woman's body on the floor. It was a black woman in a maid's dress and apron. She lay in front of a stainless steel door that had to be the elevator. I turned her to see her face. A bullet hole sat in the center of her forehead. I moved down the hall and dreaded what I would find next.

The door to Hildy's old room stood open. I called out. A shot crashed into the molding at head level.

"Hildy, it's Ace!"

Another shot.

"It's Danny!" I yelled this time.

"Danny! Help!"

The smoke reached the floor, but I saw her. Her legs extended from her torso at an awkward angle. Her skirt bunched near her waist exposing stocking-covered legs thinner than I remembered. One hand held a revolver. I ran for her and took it. Her blue eyes stared wide. A raised welt that would bruise creased her left cheek. Her blond hair erupted at all angles.

"God, thank you, thank you," she said.

I propped her against the wall to get her ready for the fireman's lift.

"I've been praying you'd get here," she moaned, and turned her head to look at me as she came off the ground.

Her fear calmed as I held her over my shoulder, but mine grew. She knew I would carry her out of the flames. Her confidence added to my fear and weakened my knees. I needed deep breaths but there were none to be had.

"Danny, get me out of here!"

One wall of her room turned orange, then the fire broke through and sucked in the air I needed.

"Danny, I'm not supposed to die!" Her fists beat my back. "Save me! You're supposed to save me!"

Smoke filled the room. I bounced her on my shoulder and she coughed. With my arm around her legs and my fingers at the top of her nylons, I staggered toward where I remembered the door should be. After five steps I adjusted my course as the doorway loomed out of the smoke. I turned into the hall and almost tripped over the dead woman. I felt Hildy tense as I swayed.

She coughed, and I held on tighter, my finger and thumb pressing hard into the back of her thigh. I felt thigh muscle ripple. I felt my way toward the stairs remembering they were close to the elevator. Three more staggering steps and I saw them. I hadn't counted steps on the way up but the house had high ceilings so I guessed at least twenty treads before the landing.

I started down. At twenty I slowed and tentatively felt each step. If I fell I would lose her and she would roll to the bottom.

"Faster, Danny!"

Her words and how she said them reminded me of other times. Now yesterday's passion and today's fear melded in my mind as I reached the second floor landing. The need to set her down became a silver-tongued snake in my mouth.

I gritted my teeth and my feet moved. After five steps, with fresh air no more than thirty feet away, my body rebelled. My sight dimmed. My brain stopped issuing orders. I caught my heel on the edge of a stair. If the railing hadn't been in my left hand I would have lost Hildy. She screamed as my grip turned me to the rail crashing her legs into the supports of the bannister.

"Ow!" she screamed, but a wracking cough further endangered my hold on her. I had to take the hand off the banister to pull her back on the shoulder. I started to lose my balance with nothing to hold on to and sat hard on the stairs.

Hildy sobbed between coughs. I found more air sitting, and drew some in.

"There's more air down here," I yelled.

She kept coughing as I rolled her onto her side, then on to her back.

"What are you doing?" she demanded.

"I'm going to drag you."

"The hell you are! You'll kill me!"

I got my arms under her shoulders, lifted, then bounced and dragged her feet toward the front door. She yelled each time her feet crashed into the next stair tread.

I looked over my shoulder. Fire encircled the door frame but the opening promised escape. I took the last three steps. When I cleared the last stair, the fire shrieked again. I whipped around, fear tightening in my stomach.

Flames closed the door opening.

I screamed and froze.

"Don't let me die!" Hildy cried again.

My feet did not move.

"Move it! Goddamn it, Danny! Don't be a coward."

I dropped her.

"What are you doing?" she screamed. "I'm sorry! I didn't mean it!"

I took three steps toward the door, then turned back. Her feet scratched for traction, thinking I'd left her. She saw me looking and grabbed her legs with her hands.

I took her under her shoulders again and pulled. By the time I hit the fire-filled doorway I had momentum. The top of my head burned as if my hair had burst into flame. We were out of the house but still under the porte cochere that showered us with embers. With ten feet to go my body quit and I sagged to my knees.

"Danny! We're close! Breathe, breathe! You can do it!"

I heard a cracking as a beam split above our heads. It would fall on us. I reached for her, caught a handful of dress and hair, and pulled her as I crawled toward safety. The beam broke free. When it hit, it sprayed embers on us. I kept my grip on her and drove with my feet as coals burned into my back.

A hard rain had begun, and I threw her to the ground as strands of her hair burned and her dress smoked. I leapt on top. We rolled on the lawn outside the portico. Each time my weight topped her she grunted, but the rain falling and the already wet ground soothed and cooled our hot spots.

I let go of her and rolled onto my back. The rain washed my face. I didn't care when the water filled my mouth and made me gag. I finally turned my head and looked at her. She looked back. With her angry face, she did not look like a grateful woman saved from certain death.

Sirens sounded down the hill. I stood.

"Don't you dare leave me, Danny," Hildy commanded.

I ignored her and staggered down the driveway into the street. Despite every porch light on the street being on, no curious citizens had braved the night. No one lurked near the crash. The shooter I'd blown off the running board hung pinned to a hedge. His hat had disappeared. White skin broke the black of his face and the hairline with its straight brown hair. I rubbed the black on the back of his hands and my fingers came away streaked black.

At the car, the driver had gone through the windshield. Blood covered glass and metal.

"What's going on out here?" A man in a bathrobe with a newspaper on his head stood on the sidewalk, pointing at the wreck. A laurel hedge across the front of his yard had blocked his view. "What happened to my tree? My God, my father planted that - "

"Shut up!" I yelled. "These men are dead and your neighbor's house is on fire, and you're whining about a tree!"

He was close enough to see the body on the hood.

"Oh, my god, my god! That poor man! Is he - "

"Of course he's dead. There's another dead man full of holes pinned in your hedge. Now go back in, call the police and make sure no one else comes out."

"Who are you? Don't tell me what to . . ."

"If you don't stop her, your wife will come out and see this. If you have kids they will, too."

"Sure, sure." He stared open mouthed at the body. "I don't want my wife to see this."

He looked again before staggering away. He retched before he could hide behind the hedge. I went back to the wreck.

The driver's torso hung through the window with his hands next to his heavily damaged head. The right hand with its broken wrist laid white palm twisted out. I looked closer at the face. Blood and other damage had ravaged the features, but the black shoe polish had come off in the crash.

I went back to the guy in the hedge. The double-ought took him in the upper body and face. He would be harder to identify than the driver. I patted his suit coat for a wallet. Nothing, but in the pocket with his cigarettes I found a matchbook from the Lullaby. I wondered why. Anyone close enough to see the matches would know this guy was as white as Uncle Sam. I kept the matches and missed my pocket. As I bent to retrieve the book I realized the guy had forgotten part of his job. He was supposed to drop them where they would have been found.

As the sirens grew near, I forced my heavy legs back to Hildy. She saw me and reached for my hand.

"Help me get away, Danny!"

"From what?" I asked, and leaned near her. "You're out of the house. The guys who did it are dead in the street. You're safe."

"Dead? Are you sure?" Her words and tone didn't fit.

"They're dead. Why? Were they supposed to get away?"

Her eyes ran through a range of emotion. I looked back at the house now totally involved with flames shooting high above the roof. Without me she would have been long and painfully dead instead of gasping air here on the lawn, so why did I feel set up?

"I don't want them to take me to the hospital," Hildy said.

"Because they'll find out you can walk?"

"Damn you! Don't let them take me!"

"You lied to the Judge about us. He spread the word and the whole town thinks I had a free pass with you. Why'd you do that?"

"It worked for both of us! People thought you were a bad ass, and I hate that son-of-a-bitch for what he did to me."

"What did he do? You can move your legs."

"Ha! I can wiggle my legs! I can't walk. I can't do anything like a real woman! So I lied. Sue me!"

"You got guts, Hildy, I'll give you that, setting fire to your own house."

"You were always dependable, Danny! Always!"

"What if I'd been a little later? Could you get out?"

She looked at her legs and said nothing.

The first fire engine came into sight a block away. It stopped far enough away not to be hit by flaming debris. A fireman ran to us.

"How bad?" he asked, and dropped beside her.

"Pretty bad," I said. "She's a cripple. You'll have to carry her out to the street so you can ship her to the hospital."

He waved for help. He tried covering her legs by pulling her skirt down.

"Don't worry about that," I said.

He gave me a funny look. "You don't look so good either. This your house?"

"I'm okay. It's Judge Bell's. This is his wife. What are you going to do?"

"With the house? Watch it burn. There's no water pressure up this high. We'll stop the spread. That's about it."

Hildy hit my arm with a fist.

"Hey! What about me?"

"I'll send flowers."

She glared at me, but said nothing.

I walked to my car. Four other fire trucks worked their way closer, and behind them I heard the higher pitched screech of an ambulance.

I wondered where the Judge was. And Birdlegs, too.

"That's my car," I called, pointing. "I'll move it."

I backed out and turned around and got past the fire trucks, then kept going. Questions were on the way that I couldn't answer. The flames had broken through the roof and tore at the night. It was a sight I'd seen before. It was a fire I'd lived through before. It was a rescue I'd made before.

The trip down went faster. I saw two more fire trucks racing up the hill and an ambulance taking its time. No rush for the dead guys and, one way or the other, Hildy would be gone. I found a booth to make a call. I dropped a nickel and called the Lullaby.

129

Birdlegs answered.

"How come you answered?" I asked.

"That what you really want to know, Ace?"

"The Judge's house is burning," I said. "How about the Lullaby?"

"Not yet. Too bad about the Judge's place. Nice house. Who did it?"

"They're dead. Hit a tree. They had black shoe polish on their faces and hands. I found a matchbook from the Lullaby in one of their pockets. I'm guessing he forgot to drop it."

"Not too smart, huh?"

"He was ducking buckshot. Probably lost track of his priorities. What's going on over there?"

"Get off the phone. I need to call in some reinforcements. Somebody hits the Judge then I'm next. Speaking of, what happened to him?"

"Not home."

"You get Hildy out?"

"Yeah. She didn't say thanks."

Birdlegs hung up.

My car didn't want to start. The starter ground until I almost abandoned hope, then it caught. We made it the mile to the garage. I told the attendant it needed work. He suggested a merciful date with the wrecking ball.

I walked three blocks to Frills, and caught Maxine on her last show. She saw me at the bar. As she left the stage she waved, and I followed her. She stopped and waited in the hall. I stepped into the light.

"Jesus!" She looked closer at my damage. "You need more than I can do."

"I'm okay," I said.

"Yeah. Come in anyway." She opened the door to the dressing room. Four women in various stages of changing clothes looked up. Two smiled and two waved. Max asked, "Who's got some burn ointment?"

A tall blond in bra and panties at the back laughed. "Who'd you get too close to, Ace?"

"Hey, this ain't funny," a short red head minus her bra said as she saw my face. "You don't look so good."

Max pushed me onto a bench while they all searched their purses. Next they went through the dressing tables. From a collection of tubes and jars, Max opened a tube and dabbed something cold and oily on my face and hands.

"Get out of your shirt," the red head said.

Max helped, and soon I felt hands rubbing a cream on spots that hurt. I winced, but didn't moan.

"Can't do much about your hair," Max said, "and your shirt's a goner. Louise, hand me that gauze and tape. We can clean up the worst ones, but somebody's gonna have to change them. Don't get them wet, either."

"I'll change them," the blonde in a pink bra named Judy said. "I do good first aid."

"Thanks, you all," I said, "but this is too much fuss. I heal good. Anybody have a man's shirt?"

Wearing a borrowed shirt, Maxine walked me the two blocks to my building. We moved slowly, as my legs threatened to knot with each step.

"How come," I asked, "no one minded me in the dressing room? I saw more than all the guys out front combined."

"Not the same thing. It was like walking in on your sister."

"Not sure that's true."

"Nobody minded. Out front, with that light shining up our skirt, the customer's paying to peek at what no man's supposed to see. If they hadn't paid for it, it had no meaning."

"Somebody ought to tell their wives," I said.

"It's okay to see your wife. It's only naughty when you pay for it. If you'd paid Judy twenty bucks to walk around minus her bra and do exactly what she did just now, it would have changed everything."

"It's not wrong until you pay for it?"

"Yes, and I'd be out of a job. Think about the rackets. What's everybody buying if it isn't guilty pleasures, or at least the hope of them?"

We turned into my building. She held my arm as I took the one step into the vestibule. We rang for the cage and listened to it rattle down. A few minutes later, she helped me out of the shirt and into a pajama top.

"What's your opinion of men?" I asked. "You see them every night paying good money to look up your skirt."

"Not every man is like that."

"In general."

"I'd rather trust a woman."

"Why?"

"I appreciate how she makes decisions. It's probably much the same process as mine. I have no idea how you think. Never will."

She buttoned the pajama top.

"Men are easy," I said. "Law of the jungle. Put 'em face to face they'll butt heads until one of them's dead."

"Men were the hunters," Max said. "Bring the food or starve. Win the battle or die. Pretty immediate stuff. Not women. We take the long view because it takes time to raise kids which is our end of the deal." She picked up her purse and moved toward the door. Before she opened it, she said, "Too many variables nowadays. Our decisions depend on do we have a man, a kid, a job, and what we want." She looked at me. "How do you feel?"

"I don't feel much anymore."

"Since you got shot?"

"That and since I got shot up in the war. Got lucky there, too."

"The war changed everybody. All the women I know lost men. Lovers, husbands, brothers, somebody. At the end of the war, women were grieving, but most of us had jobs and a sense of purpose. Then some lucky guys who lived – unlike ours – come home and take our jobs and our purpose. That kind of pissed off brings change even if you can't see it."

I couldn't sleep as the night kept running through my head. I'd killed two men. Who were they? Why had they been there? What lie was Hildy hiding and why? Yet, what I kept coming back to was the conversation with Max. Men and women and the differences between the two. I knew the men power brokers in town, but who were the powerful women and what were they doing?

Chapter 7

Rough hands shook me awake.

"Come on, Dan T! We gotta get out of here!"

The sentence repeated and the shaking kept up until I stirred. The hand moved and landed on a burn.

"Let go," I said, and swung at my tormentor. I hit a glancing blow against a thick arm, and the hand gripped me harder.

"Come on, Ace. Pinella just put a warrant out on you."

"Woozy."

I tried to kick the covers aside, but my legs felt tied to bags of cement. By the time I got out of bed, Woozy stood lookout with his gun in his hand. I dressed from the light in the hall.

"Why?" I asked. "What kind of warrant?"

"The kind that lets a cop shoot first. Pinella wants you dead . . . again." He held up a splayed hand and started ticking off his fingers. "There's the Judge," the index finger went down, "Birdlegs, the cops, Arnold Newman," the thumb was the last one standing, "and you, who don't seem to care if you live or die. Come on. I got a place to hide you."

He pulled me to the back stairs and we started down. The knots in my legs brought tears to my eyes. It was four flights of agony. Jesse Pugh waited by the back door. When he saw us, he waved us on. Woozy brought up the rear and we edged down the alley.

"Pugh, you're overreacting," I whispered.

Jesse looked back and shook his head. His mouth opened to answer, but an explosion sent all of us to the ground with hands over our heads waiting for a rain of debris. Nothing but dust and bits of plaster hit us.

"The interior," Woozy said.

"Your ass be airborne if we'd missed a light or two," Pugh said, as we got to our feet. "Come on. Let's hit it before your missing body gets labeled another miracle!"

I looked back at flames now belching out of first floor windows. People – the wrong people – were in there dying in agony.

We rode in Pugh's car through the night filling with sirens. The sound was becoming familiar.

"Thanks, guys," I said from the back-seat, leaning forward to pat their massive shoulders. "I couldn't have done another fire tonight."

The shipyards had stood eighty percent deserted since the end of the war. We turned off the deserted street and entered through an unmanned gate. The companies who remained did ship repair and outfitting, and used the slips closest to the river. Woozy's "place" was the operator's compartment on one of the giant cranes that had carried steel plates, engines, and whatever it took to crank out a Liberty ship in six days. When the monster worked around the clock, its four support legs had rolled on tracks. Now the crane loomed like a four-story giant in search of a beanstalk deep in the shadows of disuse. Pugh had dropped us at Woozy's '49 Packard and gone on his appointed rounds alone. Woozy parked under the beast and my eyes followed the stairs up until the top became a figment of my imagination.

"You carried Hildy down from the third floor?"

I nodded. He snorted.

"You need some help going up?" he asked.

"Slow will work."

A landing marked every twenty steps as the stairs zig-zagged their way up. We rested on each landing. Light from the dry dock a hundred yards away weakly lit our way. Woozy used a key to open the cabin's metal door. I followed him in. It smelled damp. I looked down on the water that had floated ships that, like Woozy and me, had gone to war. Before anything new got launched from here the waterway would need to be dredged, an enterprise no one wanted for fear of what would turn up.

"Close the door," Woozy said.

He moved around the large room and pulled black shades down.

"Blackout left from the war. No one will know you're here."

"Unless they see me coming or going on the stairs."

"Be sure they don't. Time to be invisible."

He scrapped a match and lit a camp lantern, then adjusted the wick until a white light cast hard shadows. A cot with army blankets hugged the wall opposite the operator's chair that faced the long-handled levers that had run the crane. A deal table with two chairs sat in the middle. No shades covered the windows facing the muck below then out to the deeper water of North River. Reflected light dimpled the water, dull in the muck, and crystalline where it turned navigable. A mile northwest of here the North and West Rivers met and became the Nah-Neek-Na again. Across the river lay a darkness so impenetrable it might have been a curtain to another world.

"Who tried to blow us up?" I asked, as we sat at the deal table.

"We don't know."

"Guess."

"I can't get free of this feeling the world ain't right."

"Go on."

"Hard to make guesses when the things I believe in, like knowing who the bosses are, I know now ain't right. The Judge and Greer are still going through the motions, playing the same games they been playing long as I can recall, but they seem as lost as I do. It's like the cops. Who's the boss? See what I mean?"

"So who wants to run Island City more than the bosses we already have?"

"The hundred dollar question, Ace."

"Let's get to basics. Who killed Melvin and why? Where's Christina? How about Hildy? Why did she take off before they got her to the hospital?"

"You think she did it on her own?"

"Nothing much wrong with her. She can walk, I don't know how well, but when she thought she was going to die, she moved her legs."

"Okay, so we're not ruling anybody out," Wozinsky said. "Your turn to guess."

"If I do will I have to explain?"

"No. Give us a wild-hair-up-your-ass kind of guess. You've always been good at those."

"Here goes. Melvin is killed because he learns something working downstairs at the A.C. The only one he might have told, Christina, is gone, too, leaving us nowhere."

"Hildy?"

"Maxine told me something that sort of plays. She says if anyone ought to be pissed about the ways things have been since the war ended it's the women. Doing good during the war, then the men come home and it's back to baby sitting with no money and no respect."

"So?"

"Back to what if. Hildy called the shots while the Judge was away. He comes home, she gets elbowed out, but Hildy misses the power. What if Melvin finds out Hildy was planning a move, tells Christina because he thinks maybe he's got an ally even if he's talking about her mother and she tells Hildy. Bye-bye Melvin. Maybe Christina took Melvin out herself and she's laying low, or she didn't like what Hildy was up to and Mom has her baby girl on ice."

Woozy leaned back in his chair and stared at me.

"Why would Melvin find out what the women were up to in the private rooms of the A.C., the holiest of holies for the men?" Woozy asked. "If the guys knew, the Judge would know."

"Maybe the basement isn't where Melvin heard. Maybe he heard something in the staff area, like the kitchens. Maybe he heard it from a maid that worked the family areas. Shit, maybe he heard on the streetcar for all we know! Maybe what he heard, by itself, didn't mean much, but with other things he dug up in his attempt to figure our old Mr. White, he stumbled onto a truth nasty enough to get him killed."

"If that's the case," Woozy said, leaning back and pushing his hat up, "you and me going to have a tough time finding what it was."

"Maybe not. Birdlegs keeps promising to help me. This is his chance. I'll get to him and tell him I need to talk to the women who worked the A.C. that Melvin could have overheard. He can set up a little meet in his office at the Lullaby."

"Birdlegs might be kinda busy," Wozinsky said. "A shooting out front of the Lullaby, but no fatalities. Birdlegs had the guns out and no one got close."

"The Judge ever show up at his smoking embers?"

"Alive and well, and pissed as hell. He's looking for you."

"No doubt to thank me for saving his wife. I need some truth. Not headlines-on-the-hour kind of truth, but cop-around-town truth. You fed me Marvin and his family, kept me in the loop on all the latest, and now here we are just you, me and Pugh. Why?"

"I got to count on you being around. Pugh and me, we're feeling real expendable. I go down, I want somebody getting even. You're the best bet."

"It's worse in the last twenty-four hours?"

"Jesse and me, we been holding back on you. Not our style to whine. Today at roll call I looked around and counted three faces I'd worked with before. A month ago I knew all but four or five. Pinella's using schedules, lay-offs, and suspensions to isolate the ones he can't push around. If Jesse and me wind up with our asses in a sling, we can't call for back-up because we don't know who to trust."

"How come he hasn't separated you guys?"

"We figure we're going to be ambushed. Two more victims of the gang war. One ambush is easier to sell than two. We plan on making you our backup."

"Awkward for the news release that the gangs in town ain't fighting," I said. "Sort of explains the Judge's house and the Lullaby shooting. What's your plan?"

"Sic you on Pinella."

"That's it?"

"It's a start. You stick a firecracker up his ass and he'll lead me to the next stop. Sort of like breaking the rack on a pool table."

"What if you're out of time?"

"Jesse and me plan to buy some. Pinella will be a couple of swinging dicks light for a day or two. We got some sick leave to use before it's a wreath on a coffin." He rocked back in his chair. "I kinda like your what-if about Hildy. I'd never given that angle a glance. Me and Jesse can do some checking."

The harsh light of the Coleman lantern either starkly illuminated or deeply shadowed the crags in his big face. It made it hard to read.

"You scared?" I asked.

"Of course I am. What kind of a fool wouldn't be? I didn't live through the war to get gunned down on my front porch."

"Where you and Pugh laying low?"

"We got a place."

"Good as this?"

"No, but you're the ace in the hole. So to speak. That footlocker over there's got a Browning Automatic Rifle, and some M-1's. The ammo boxes are full. There's a bazooka tube with four shells and some hand grenades in the closet. Lot of GI ordinance still around." He waved his arm at the cabin. "This place was built to withstand a Jap attack like Pearl. Reinforced walls and floors, but stay out of the windows. The siding will burn but you won't. Course you ain't scared of a little fire after rescuing Hildy and escaping the hotel."

He took a stack of currency out of his coat pocket and placed it on the table.

"I cleaned out the stash you keep in that drawer before I woke you," he said. "If I hadn't you'd be penniless, and an honest cop like me would have been hard pressed to finance you. Time to find a new stash hole."

I thanked him and a few minutes later he left me high above the shipyard. I watched him on the stairs from the grated walk that ringed my new home. Island City stretched to the south. The street lights of the Calder Hills traced the curving streets as they wound to the top. If the Judge's house had still been on fire, I would have seen it. Lower down, the city lights slowly sloped toward the river before they ended in blackness. I felt like a sentry walking guard duty at a remote outpost, staring into the distance hoping for a glimpse of meaning that would make whatever lay ahead important enough to die for.

I had a leg up on that sentry. I knew my mission and it was worth the risk. I was supposed to be dead, but here I stood. I wanted to know why. I wanted to know who tried to kill me almost as much as I wanted to know why I was still alive. Maybe I'm more of a man in the middle than anyone knows. The middle meaning neither one nor the other. Neither the Judge nor Birdlegs. Neither honest nor dishonest. Neither alive nor dead.

Back inside, I hit the cot. The feel of GI blankets and the musty, damp smell brought back memories of tents in the rain and the distant sound of artillery, but not for long. I slept.

I dreamed of that night in the Bulge. Me caught in the open between my forward post and our camp after being relieved. Seeing the tracers slash the night and the impact of the shells gouging earthmover-size bundles of earth out of the ground. The screams of the wounded and their sudden end as men died. The flames lighting the pitiful HQ honed out of a farmer's house and the shadows of burning men waving frantically as they gyrated past where windows had been. I ran at the fire, crashed in the door, grabbed the first man I saw, and hauled him toward the night. Back and forth

I went until the fire collapsed the ceiling. I saw the men I'd pulled out. None moved. I'd saved the already dead.

I awoke sweating, then fell down the hole into sleep again.

There are shades of black and a shade even deeper than pitch-black. I awoke into deeper black, and something still darker glided toward me. I smelled honeysuckle strong enough to overpower the musty dampness. That scent was the last thing I remembered after getting shot. Birdlegs had smelled it, too. An icy chill froze on my spine and I couldn't move. My eyes ached from staring. I felt sure a woman wearing a veil hovered above me. Besides the honeysuckle, I heard a swishing of crepe skirts as she glided to my side. I imagined the veil tickling my nose.

"What are you?" I asked.

I felt a faint breath as if a breeze blew from a great distance.

"Who are you?" I asked again.

The exhalation came again.

"Death be a lady tonight," I said, then whistled the tune to *Luck Be a Lady*.

"What is the real mystery, Danny?" came the whisper, louder now into words.

The breath came, then faded, as the honeysuckle vanished and black became just black.

Chapter 8

I woke to a hard rain. The bed clothes were soaked, and I looked for a leak in the ceiling, but it was sweat. Spring had finally arrived.

I felt worse than when I'd laid down. I blamed it on the cot, and the wartime smell and feel of the blankets. I tested the air for the scent of honeysuckle, and breathed easier when all I found were the disagreeable odors of male life haunting the crane's cabin since the war. I cracked the blackout curtains and swept the ground below with field glasses looking for anyone watching my new lair. I felt like an eagle surveying his territory in search of prey – only I was the prey. I saw no one and painfully descended to earth. I found a cab waiting for fares near a freighter in dry dock for repairs, and headed for town.

Delinda Paz, she who'd shared the frame in the picture with Christina Bell and wanted to sell information about her, lived in an apartment house respectable enough to have a self-serve elevator, but stopped short of a doorman. A nice place, but sort of like when she stood behind Christina in Dotty's picture, no one noticed her. Her place wasn't so nice it prodded close inspection. I pressed the button outside the building's door and she invited me to ride to the fifth floor. The elevator buttons said the building had six floors. I saw a theme for Delinda – not quite top rung.

She stood in her doorway, arms folded in front of her, and watched me.

"I know you," she said.

"Me or my type?"

"Both." She moved aside to let me in. "As for the latter, you have the hard, used look of a man back from war who doesn't know what to do except keep fighting. As for the former, you and I have met before."

"I doubt it. I would have remembered."

"Apparently you don't."

She closed the door and crossed her arms again as her eyes took me in.

"Get out of your clothes," she said.

"I definitely would have remembered if we'd met," I said, to cover my surprise.

"You need a shower and fresh linen. The bathroom's down the hall."

Her apartment made a statement on its own. Good art on the walls, furniture that didn't sacrifice function for form, and a subdued color scheme that said she wasn't afraid to be the star of her own home. Venetian blinds reduced the outside light to regular slats of light and dark. I had to rethink her.

"Tell me about that hard, used look," I said.

"Look in the mirror lately?"

"Only when I can't avoid it."

"You know the look. War strips away the memory that there's more to life than your next breath."

"How do you know? A keen observer?"

"I was there."

"Then you're older than you look."

"Aren't we all?"

Her frankness invited inspection. I looked at her closer, choosing her green eyes as the best place to begin.

"May I sit?"

"Not until after the shower. You smell. I have your size."

Ten minutes later she came into the bathroom while I was toweling. She looked at my naked body and indicated I should turn in place. I did and felt her eyes all over me.

"Like I said, Dan T., you have that hard, used look. Ever count the bullet holes? What are the bigger scars? Shrapnel?"

"Yeah. I had a bad war."

She still wore the satin day robe she'd met me in. Her frank examination of me was not that of a sister or a mother, more like a nurse or a doctor.

"Think you can go on forever with those holes in you?"

Right to the point of it all. I appreciated the opening.

"I'd rather not," I replied staring into the green eyes looking for some truth, or maybe a hand up the ladder to get closer to the truth.

I finished dressing in the fresh clothes she provided. Everything fit like it was out of my drawer – if I had a drawer. I followed her down the hall to the living room. She pointed at a chair. "Legs tired from carrying Hildy?"

Gravity already had me, or I would have stopped to stare.

"How do you know?"

"Not much happens in Island City I don't know about."

She waited until I sat, then leaned on an elbow against the mantle above a dark fireplace. The pose accentuated the enticing curves of her figure. It was a test to see if her obvious charms would distract me.

"I've always been a sucker for green eyes," I said. She smiled and moved toward the settee. "Since you tested me, I'll test you. Who's Arnold Newman?"

"There is no Arnold Newman."

"That's it? Case closed?"

"Almost." She sat across from me and took her time smoothing her robe over her long and shapely thighs. "Did

Dotty Orland tell you I'm her best source? I always seem to be in the right place at the right time."

Now she met my eyes and I sat straighter. I sensed my being here was no accident, examined the feeling, and felt sure I'd been here before. She smiled as my thoughts appeared on my face. With her smile I saw her change. It was as if she assumed a new inner identity with no more than a slight shiver on the outside, the kind of shiver you might make as you passed into the twilight zone.

"What are you really trying to learn?" she asked, her voice soft and melodic, her posture both relaxed and focused. My eyelids drooped as I listened to her. I shook my head.

"From you?" I asked.

"Let's start with a bigger picture. Overall, what do you want to know?"

"I want to know what happened to Melvin Jackson, and where Christina Bell is."

"What's in it for you if you do?" she asked.

"Money. The satisfaction of a job well done."

"And that's it? Is it enough? More to the point, is that what you really want, or is it just a superficial copout to keep you from looking deeper? Maybe hide the ignorance you feel?"

"I'm tired of ignorance. Ignorance gets led around by its nose just like you're doing to me right now."

She put a hand on my knee.

"Would you like a clue?" she asked.

"A real clue or just more nose pulling?"

"A real clue, but one not easy to read."

"As long as you promise it's a real clue, go for it."

"It's real. This is it. What's the most stable form in nature?"

"It's a clue masquerading as a geometry quiz. Goody."

"The answer to this 'quiz' is your answer to everything."

I looked at her and suffered another "been-here-done-that" moment. It was more than the *déjà vu* moments I'd been having.

"Where do I start?" I asked.

"What have you learned so far?"

"There's always been a balance between the Judge and Birdlegs. Now chaos could break the balance. If it does, I don't know who would profit."

"Are you sure you don't know? Wouldn't you profit? They call you the man in the middle."

"I don't know what the middle is anymore. Jackson, the Judge, and Birdlegs all want to know what's really happening. And how do you know I carried Hildy down the stairs?"

"She didn't walk, and you were there. A fireman saw you carrying her." She smiled. "And Hildy told me you were coming at ten o'clock."

"Do you and Hildy talk often?"

"As needed. She's called often since Christina left."

"Left? Sounds benign when the possible reason she's missing include murder. Unless you know something."

"I know how to make Hildy feel better without lying to her."

"I was thinking more like you know where Christina is."

"If I did I could tell her father and collect the fee he's offered you."

"Maybe you don't need the money," I said, looking around the room.

"We are running away from your geometry test," she said. "Do you know the answer?"

"No! I got a C in geometry! I came to ask about Christina. I saw the picture with you and her together at a dance at the A.C."

I was running and she knew it. I professed a desire for the truth, but when hints of what it may be peeked at me, I hid. I stood and paced despite the pain in my legs.

"You want to ask me why I had my picture taken with Christina," she said. "Is that the most important thing you want to know?"

"No."

"What is?"

I got up and walked around looking at framed photographs of people I didn't recognize, picked up an ornate glass ashtray with a family crest etched in the bottom, and looked at a table lamp with a tasseled shade and an odd switch. It looked familiar.

"I feel like I've been here before," I said, images dancing in my head as if clawing their way to the surface of my awareness.

"Bravo," she said, and clapped while her eyes shone. "How wonderful."

"What's so wonderful?"

"You have never remembered before."

"How many times have I been here?"

"My dear," she said, and pointed at the chair again, "my role is not to answer questions. My role is to encourage you to *ask* them."

"Your role? Do I have one?"

Her smile grew and she clapped her hands again, but she said nothing. Her expression suggested I try again.

"Who assigns the roles?"

She took my hands in hers and squeezed. "This is very encouraging."

"Maybe for you, but it's pissing me off."

"Do not let your frustration fog your mind. It will only make it worse."

"Is this Hell?"

"I can answer that one. No. What do you really want to ask me?"

I did not want to ask that question. Even if she didn't answer it could tell me something I didn't want to know.

"Be brave," she whispered. "You won't be sorry you asked."

"How do you know?"

"That is not the question."

"Did I die when I got shot?"

"That's the question!" She squeezed my hands again. "Think of all you've learned today."

"I've learned nothing."

She squeezed again. "You phrased that perfectly."

"Because I didn't ask it as a question?"

"Perfectly. Now you know the most important questions. What's next?"

"Look for their answers."

"Exactly! Then what?"

"Maybe the most important answers provide an answer to more than one question."

"It's a place to start," she said, and stood.

"Will I be back?"

She tilted her head and raised an eyebrow.

I rephrased it. "I hope I come back some day."

She clapped her hands with a sparkle in her eyes. She kissed my cheek and said, "I'm sure we'll meet again."

She followed me to the door. I stopped, and she had to walk around me to open it. When I didn't move she looked at me.

"I want to learn something," I said, "but the phrasing is elusive."

"Be patient. Think clearly."

I held up my hand and said, "You strike me as a woman who wears honeysuckle perfume."

She smiled, opened the door, and pushed me out.

"I wear honeysuckle, but not all the time. It is a very feminine scent."

Even though she pushed, I stopped with my foot in her door. "I was actually good at geometry," I said. "The answer to your quiz is the triangle."

She stared at me and a slight smile curved the corner of her mouth.

"Next clue. Do you know what spiritual transcendence means?"

"No, and that's the truth."

"Seek an answer, Dan T."

As I turned, she took my arm.

"One more thing. This is not a world for answers, but for questions. Like the meaning of death and life." She smiled at me as she lowered her chin. She was Lauren Bacall looking up at Bogie. "Never quit seeking, Dan T."

Now she even sounded like Bacall.

The door closed. The lock engaged.

Most of Island City's upper middle class, defined as those who failed to scramble their way into the rarefied air of the Calder Hills, lived on the west side of downtown in a crotch formed by the hills and the West River. The main current of the Nah-Neek-Na swung wide of the West River and swept around the tip of Island City and became the North. The West had been formed by a giant flood that had notched the far side and created an island out of a peninsula long before inhabitants arrived. The bedrock on the far side turned the river northward, the current carrying the commercial river traffic toward the ocean while the placid back waters of the West served mostly pleasure boats. The prevailing winds blew from the west and spared this part of town any noxious industrial odors. Pleasant houses with white fences and fresh paint said it was a nice place to live and raise a family. Gino Pinella had sold his soul to do just that.

At eleven o'clock I stood down the street in the shadow of a tree and watched the last light in the Pinella house go out. I gave the family another hour to get settled and asleep before picking the lock on the back door. There was no chain. A police officer lived here.

I'd been in the house once before and remembered my way around. I went into his den at the foot of the stairs and turned on the console radio next to his desk. Big band swing played and echoed through the house. Five minutes went by before the light on the stairs came on. I checked to make sure it was him then moved behind the door. I heard the slap of his slippers. His arm pointing a revolver cleared the door, then the rest of him. When he stood in the room, I stepped close, gripped his gun and twisted it out of his hand. He yelped.

"Shut up, Gino," I said.

"Wh . . who?" he stuttered.

"Sit on your desk and be quiet. We don't want the family coming down now, do we?"

"Ace!" He looked over his shoulder trying to see in the gloom as I pushed him onto the desk.

"Alive and well. At least well enough to bury you. Hands behind your head."

He gave resistance a valiant passing thought then did as ordered. I turned the radio off and the desk lamp on.

"Time to play truth or consequences, Gino."

"I have nothing to say to you, Spader. You're a wanted fugitive. If you're smart you'll turn yourself over to me. I'll be sure you get a square shake."

"So I got nothing to lose if I put a slug between your eyes?" I pointed his gun at his head.

Panic flooded his face and he thought about what he'd said.

"You're not a murderer. I mean you're not wanted for murder. You'd be a fool to kill a policeman."

"Killing you and killing a cop ain't the same thing."

The panic opened the floodgates on his sweat glands. Water ran down his high forehead.

"You can't be happy about the cop turnover, Gino. Used to be if someone wanted to buy a cop it meant you. That's how you got this house. I'll bet all the competition you got now hurts. Falling behind on your mortgage?"

The sweat reached his eyes and a hand came up to wipe them. I slapped it away.

"Answer a question and wipe your eyes," I said. "Who's pulling your strings?"

"What if I tell you?"

"Good question. I'm going to ask a question twice. You tell me the first time and I walk out the door and tell no one. You tell me the second time, I say you talked and they kill you. You don't tell me and I still say you did, then wait to see who kills you. Um, sounds like it's either dead or alive. Your choice."

The sweat streamed into his eyes.

"Go ahead," I said. "Wipe your eyes. It's the last break you get."

He dabbed at his face with the sleeve of his striped pajamas.

"Gino, I'm doing you a favor. I could have spread the rumor and you'd already be ducking bullets. Who's making the changes in the cops?"

Even through his fear, Pinella held my eyes. If I pulled the trigger he wanted to see the bullet coming.

"I don't know. You can tell anyone anything you want, but no one will believe you. They know I don't know. Orders come from the chief just like always and I follow them. I'm flattered you'd think I was in on it."

The sweat slowed as he put his truth on the table. It was a hard truth. Not only had he admitted he wasn't a player, but his fear had nothing to do with talking. He feared me.

"You thought I came to kill you, didn't you?"

"Yes."

"Because I wanted to or because I was sent?"

"You hate me."

"Do most people in the cops think I kill people because I hate them?"

"We know you kill people."

I looked around his den with its books and paintings. It was the room of an educated man. I compared it to Joshua Jackson's. Other than the chess board and the picture of Jesus, they shared similarities.

"Sit still, Gino." I put his gun in my coat pocket. "Let's talk. What's your plan? Long-term. You want to hang on to the dream? House, family, and live happily ever after?"

"I'm trying. I got five kids. They all need an education."

"Being a dirty cop is going to get them there?"

"You know anybody in this town who has both money and their dignity?"

"How long you counting on this lasting? Ten, fifteen years?"

"More."

"You won't make it. There's a storm coming, and you'll get washed away. The old guard – probably including most of your better customers – is scared. Birdlegs, the Judge. They don't know who's moving in. You're dumbing down the cops to make them useless. Guys like Wozinsky and Pugh are digging trenches and cleaning their ammo. They see it. Reminds them of the Pacific and Anzio. They made it through that war and now they're wondering why."

"That's been a few years."

"Spoken like a man who wasn't there. It was yesterday. It will always be yesterday."

"What about you? You're here, too."

"I guess. Maybe this is Hell. I take it a day at a time."

"I would never have picked you for a philosopher. You keep going because that's what you do. Right? Very existential."

"If that makes me a philosopher, then yes. What are you going to do, Gino?"

"Same as you. Hope for the best."

"I do more than hope. Make the best happen. Join the side of the angels."

"And that's you?"

"This town ain't much, but it's ours, so we fight. It's that or leave. You make the right choice then you listen and think about what you hear. Remember who you see. Never ask why, and use your brain. No one will notice if you don't ask why. We'll find ways to pass the word."

"What if I'm lying now?"

"You're not. You sweat when you're afraid and when you lie. Right now you're not sweating."

I put his gun on his desk and walked away.

"I could kill you right now," he said, and I heard the click of the hammer locking.

I sniffed the air and checked the corners. No honeysuckle. No woman in black deepening the shadows.

"You won't."

As I walked through the shadow of Island City, easy in that part of town with its high trees leafing out in the sudden warmth of the delayed spring, I wondered if I'd made a bad assumption about the woman in the veil. What if she wasn't death? Back in the crane when I dreamed her, or saw her, I didn't die. I smelled the honeysuckle on Birdlegs's floor, and didn't die there either. What if she was my guardian? Can't call her an angel in her black-on-black, but my literal interpretations gave me something to think about as I walked toward the lights of downtown. Where the trees and their shadows gave out, the streetcar tracks started. I walked in the street without traffic and stepped on the running board of a tram when it ground passed.

I needed answers to hard questions; facts instead of philosophical puzzles. That meant Maxine's role got bigger since she could walk the streets in the light of day and I couldn't. Thanks to the warrant, I needed her ear to either confirm or deny any tidbit Pinella might pass along. It was too late to find her at Frills, so I tried the Virginia.

A lone woman left the café while I was a half block away. She looked upscale for the Virginia with a mid-calf skirt, heels, and a dark beret on the back of her head, but she walked like Max. I started to call to her and then saw the two men across the street and a hundred feet ahead of her. She might be working so I hung back. The men turned at the next corner and she didn't. She bought a cab at the stand outside the Diamond Hotel, and so did I. The magic words, "Follow that cab" brought a smile to the driver's face.

The empty streets kept me well back of her cab. I saw it stop outside the high-rise Envoy Apartments. She got out, and talked to the doorman. Not many apartment houses had doormen, and even fewer doormen had backup to talk your way by before passing through the revolving door. Maybe she was expected because she waved and entered.

"Drive by slow," I told my hack driver.

On closer look, the backup belonged to the Judge.

"So that's where he is," I muttered.

When we were clear, I paid off the cab and started around the block on foot. The back of the building had men watching, too, so I didn't make the turn and added more miles to my shoe leather. I wondered how many others used these well protected luxury digs as a place to hole up. By the time I found another cab my legs were dreading the stairs I faced at the crane.

The question on the ride to the dry dock boiled down to: What was Max doing at the Envoy?

I dropped the cab by the freighter in for repairs. The shadows swallowed me well before I reached the stairs.

Chapter 9

I read the lunch menu sitting at Giga's counter. The same guys that had reached for hard boiled eggs and pickled pig's feet when this case started still reached. Virgil Wozinsky hadn't come in yet, but I had hopes. A reserved card sat on his usual table which meant he'd called ahead. When Woozy and Pugh came through the door, Woozy saw me and pointed at their table.

"What's new?" I asked, while they pulled out chairs.

"Crime's up," Pugh said, as usual.

"You see Yes-sir?" Woozy asked as he levitated his ass to pull the chair closer to the table. He looked at Pugh.

"The shit," Pugh said, and Woozy nodded, completing the ritual.

"I saw him."

"I figured you did because he looked at me funny this morning."

"Yeah, me too," Pugh added, leaning away so Pearl could pour coffee. "At least you didn't kill him, Ace. I would have."

Pearl didn't spill a drop, and I wondered at the range of conversations she overheard. I doubted she listened.

"Pinella thinks he has more in common with you guys," I said, "than with the new regime."

"Bullshit," Woozy said.

"The shit," Jesse added.

"He says he doesn't know who's calling the shots. He even thanked me for thinking anyone would confide in him."

Woozy looked at me and raised an eyebrow.

"That sounds like the truth," he said.

"I wouldn't tell him shit," Jesse said.

"As far as he's concerned, nothing's changed. The chief tells him what to do and he says 'Yes-sir.' Not his choice of words."

"What're you thinking?" Woozy asked. He turned away and looked at Pearl. "Give me two blue plates."

She wrote then looked at me.

"Grilled cheese and a piece of lemon pie."

She left and I looked at Pugh.

"His turn to order," he said, and pointed at Woozy.

"I think Pinella's telling the truth," I said. "I never considered it until he thanked me. I figure he's staying alive because an ass-kisser as dependable as him is hard to find. But he's scared. He's glimpsing a tomorrow where kissing ass won't be enough."

"Could be," Woozy said. "What's he going to do?"

"We'll find out. I told him to keep his ears open and ask no questions. We know he'll keep his head down so maybe we'll learn something."

"Anybody know who we going to be shooting at yet?" Pugh asked.

"No," I said. "You guys?"

"I got a real bad feeling," Woozy said. "Like in the war when it got too quiet and all you could hear was the sound of your sphincter slammin' shut."

"The bullets start flying," Jesse said, leaning forward, "stay off my left side. Okay?"

"Why?" I asked.

"In the war, three times the guy on my left took it between the eyes. One a week for three weeks. In Italy."

"What happened before Italy?" I asked.

"Nothing. Those guys was scrawny, but bang and down they went. Look at me. I look like a tank. How do you miss a tank? It still bothers me, so stay off my left. If Yes-sir fights with us we'll put him there."

Pearl arrived with lunch for five. When I saw the plates I realized Woozy's "two blue plates" was an order for two each. Each of their plates had stacks of corn beef on rye surrounded by sauerkraut and green beans. She squeezed my diminutive plate with one grilled cheese and a smaller plate for the lemon pie around the edges of the table. As I leaned away to avoid the flying food, I took the pie with me. If I didn't eat it first I wouldn't get a taste.

Conversation died while the food vanished one mammoth mouthful at a time. When Jesse finished he looked at my empty pie plate and shook his head. Pearl came back with coffee.

"Ace says the pie's real good today," Jesse said to her. "Better bring me one."

"You want the whole pie or just a piece?"

He and Woozy exchanged looks and Pearl left without a spoken word.

"You still got that bad feeling?" I asked Woozy.

"Like a fish on the end of a line. I'd start shooting if I knew where to aim."

"I think I know where the Judge is," I said.

Pearl set a pie tin minus one piece on the debris left from the last course. Jessie cut the remainder in half and pushed the tin where they could both reach it.

"The Envoy," Woozy said, waving his fork.

"How'd you know?" I asked.

Pugh used his fork to cut off a hunk of lemon pie. The meringue atop the curd shimmered like an avalanche choosing its moment.

"You ain't the only one working," Pugh said, as he delicately balanced the fork load toward his mouth. The pie made a clean entry other than traces of meringue in the corners. "He's got to be somewhere. Not like he can go home."

"Hildy?" I asked.

"Still among the missing. You gotta wonder if she and Christina are missing together."

"I feel like we're losing ground," I said. "Instead of finding answers we're finding questions."

"Losing sight of priorities, too," Woozy said, "When's the last time you talked to Joshua Jackson?"

"I got nothing to tell him." They each had a bite of pie left. They waited until they each forked their bite and ended lunch in synch. "Maybe the reason we aren't seeing anyone new in town is that there isn't. Maybe we have a familiar face in a new role."

"Like?" Woozy asked with his mouth full.

"Like who ran the town during the war? Every able body was in uniform. Was the Judge here? I know Birdlegs wasn't. He didn't show up until the war was almost over."

"He tell you that?" Woozy asked.

"Yeah. Makes sense, though. When you hit town, Jesse?"

"After the war. My old lady moved here from Texas in '42 to work in the yards. She made it through a racial disturbance down south and came north."

"Birdlegs had nobody to prey on until the shipyards brought more black people. The war ends, the wives who worked the yards are here, so the men show. Perfect set-up for Birdlegs."

"I don't know anybody who lived here before the war," Pugh said.

"The Jacksons did," Woozy said, "and this was a white bread kind of town. Ace, these questions are great while my lunch gets settled, but we ain't gettin' no place. The Judge is holed up in the Envoy. Birdlegs says he don't know any more about what's going on than we do, and Marvin worked down in the gaming rooms at the A.C. which doesn't help us a bit."

"Hey, don't forget the warrant out on Ace," Jesse said.

"Yeah, what's that all about?" I asked. "I was asleep when you picked me up and I don't remember asking. This about the fire?"

"The warrant said 'Material witness to an event of interest,' but nobody's looking very hard," Woozy said, digging in a coat pocket. He came up with a toothpick. "Jesse, the only thing all this stuff has in common is Ace here. What are you doing that has people scared, Ace? What do you want?"

"I want to know who killed Marvin Jackson."

"No," Woozy said, waving the toothpick. "What do you really want?"

How come people kept asking me this? First Delinda Paz and now Woozy. Yesterday the philosophical fork in the road came as a distraction, so today I kept my answer a simple, "That's it. Just who killed Marvin?"

"You're a guy, what, thirty-five years old, and there's nothing you want?" Woozy said accusatorially. "Start thinking about the answer, because I want to know."

"What difference does it make? So what if I'm just a guy who made it through the war, doesn't feel like finding a wife, and muddles along on his own?"

"You're not one of the guys, Ace. Listen to me." Woozy reached across the table dragging a cuff through the remainder of lunch to touch my wrist. "You are the guy who died. You didn't have a brush with death. You died. I saw you in the morgue with a sheet over your head. I pulled it back to take a look at my partner and felt sad and angry. You lay there for a couple of hours, and then you sat up and said, Where am I? Got a clue as to how I'm supposed to deal with that?"

He gripped my wrist tighter.

"Jesse, in the war, how many guys you see get shot dead?" Woozy asked.

"Hundreds. Maybe thousands."

"Any of them get up and walk away?"

Jesse shook his head, his eyes locked on me.

"On some of those Pacific atolls," Woozy said, "I saw Jap bodies stacked up like cord-wood. None of them came back."

He let go of me to light a Chesterfield.

"That night after you got shot, I talked to Birdlegs. He said you died in his arms. You stopped breathing, and went still. Ace, you touched dead guys before. You can tell from the touch exactly the moment they die. That was you. Then you stood up and walked away."

162

Jessie sat staring at me while Woozy smoked.

"I told you Jesse and I pulled some volunteer guard duty while you were in the hospital. We wanted to see who'd visit you. Seeing how you rose from the dead, we figured God or maybe the pope. Instead it's a couple of goons with death wishes. Who are you and what are you doing here?"

They both stared at me waiting for an answer. The intensity of their stares forced me to look for an answer that would tell us all something.

"My memory's a little frazzled from before," I finally said. "Kinda like a deck of cards getting shuffled. All the memories are there but not in the right order."

"You don't know what happened, do you?" Woozy said. "I told you, Jesse."

"Told him what?" I asked.

"That you'd be clueless. So here's a little chronology for you. You get shot you're dead for a few hours." He held his finger up, then lowered it to point at me like you'd take aim with a gun. "Then you come back to life. For three weeks you're in the hospital, then one day you're gone. Checked out. Where'd you go?"

"You guys are scaring me," I said truthfully. "I'm nothing special. I got lucky. Weird stuff happens."

"You gotta a kind of weird all your own," Jesse said. "My pastor – and yeah, I got one – say we all got to be on the lookout for apocalyptic events. He ain't talking the end of the world shit. No, he called it a paradigm shift. Like when the dead start not being dead. Like Christ. Maybe you're the new Christ, but I hope not."

"Let's get back to the chronology," Woozy said. "You get shot and you're gone eight months. Then I see you walking down the street heading for the Virginia Café. We have dinner and it's like you've never been gone. You look a little gaunt, but all in all, you look real good for a dead guy. I ask you how long you've been back and where you're back from, but you shrug and tell me you like not being a cop."

"Own kind of weird, uh huh," Jesse said.

Pearl patted Woozy on the shoulder. "We got to go?" he asked her.

"You got a call at the bar," she said.

"Ace, you think about this until I catch up with you again," Woozy said as he spilled change for a tip on the table. "How many people ain't scared to be alone with you?"

"Other than us," Jesse said as Woozy went to answer the phone, "but even I keep my eye on you. How about you, Pearl? You afraid of Ace?"

"Nah. He's cute. Not enough cute guys around. Besides, after what I saw in Austria at the end of the war, nothing much scares me. At least when I'm awake."

"What you'd do in Austria?" I asked.

"Secretary for some general trying to get rich in black market penicillin and Lucky Strikes. He always volunteered to be first into an area so he could piss in the corners. His staff had to go along. We were in a car that hit a mine. I was the only one who made it."

"Now you're pouring mud for Giga," I said.

"I love it," she said, pushing a wisp of gray hair out of her eyes. "Chance to stop and smell the bacon. Feels right."

She and her coffee-pot left us. As Jesse watched her, he said to me, "I hate phone calls like that," and pointed at Wozinsky's back. "Me and Woozy are thinking our date with an ambush is getting closer."

"Any reason in particular?"

"Us out of the way and there ain't any real street cops left."

"Not to wish you ill or anything, but what's holding them back?"

"Two schools of thought. Woozy thinks it's his arsenal. We ain't the easiest targets to take down. Me, I think it's you. They hit us and not you, you're going to be a pain in the ass."

Woozy hung up and waved.

"So it's better to hit us all at the same time," I said.

"Yep. You might start thinking about a good place to make a stand."

The muggy afternoon, a legacy of dense low clouds and warm temperatures that sucked moisture out of the waterlogged earth, tempted me to forego my plans to track down William I. Travis, the photographer who took the picture of Christina and Melvin at the Lullaby. The temptation died when I remembered the warnings I'd heard lately about the tenuous nature of life. I flagged a cab.

The address I'd copied off the back of the photo Dotty Orland had bought from Travis gave his address as Terminal Four and a building number. If a photographer needed cheap space, one of the old wartime terminals was an ideal location. Especially if he wanted some privacy – not much class, but lots of privacy. The cab dropped me at an unmanned guard shack. I pushed open a wire gate held closed by a brick, and explored.

Terminal Four was one of six huge, largely abandoned terminal complexes on the North River. Each in its day had stored materiel bound for a theater of war. Liberty ships, made right here in Island City, were pulled by tug to one of the many wharves where the ship's holds were crammed with what was needed at the front. Since peace broke out, the decaying warehouses, most at least two blocks long and all needing paint, begged for tenants.

More chain link separated the street from the terminals' outside storage area. Tarpaulins draped over lumps of various sizes suggested machinery that was either stored against a future war, or intended for peaceful purposes whose use had disappeared with time. The tarps cinched at the waist with rope created folds that had become home to healthy fields of algae, and the faded canvas convinced me they'd sat in the yard for years. Stacks of pallets and metal drums added to the abandoned clutter.

I found stenciled numbers in black paint over the big sliding doors on the end of each warehouse. Too bad I hadn't found them sooner. Including the two hundred yards I'd spent taking the wrong direction, I walked a half mile before I found the right number. The upside was I had a good overview of the complex. At one point I visited the river side and confirmed it was more of the same with draped pallets stacked against the warehouse walls. I stared across the river at the far side lost in its fog bank. More tree stumps and debris usually found on land floated in the dirty water, and with more urgency than the last time I'd noticed.

Outside the last warehouse in the row sat an old Ford with its driver-side door open. The number on the warehouse matched Travis's address. I looked inside the car and found keys under the front seat, but nothing else. Either someone had cleaned it out or there was no reason to lock the door. I checked the steering column for the registration. The card confirmed Travis as the owner.

A human-sized entrance sat as an inset in the larger loading door. Both doors were locked, but a key from the ring did the trick on the smaller one. The humidity inside felt and smelled enough like a jungle to evoke war memories of the Pacific if Woozy ever visited. Fog clouded the upper reaches of the ceiling, filtering light from the high windows. Puddles of water scattered around the floor. It felt damp enough inside to rain.

A row of low plasterboard offices lined the wall on the side away from the river. On the first door I found Travis's business card nailed to the door. As the door opened it unleashed the smell of death. My nose wrinkled and my stomach clenched. I pushed the door all the way open to let the smell dissipate even though I knew it would do little good. I made no effort to turn on a light.

I went to the outer door in the next office. It opened and more of the fetid air escaped. From the doorway it appeared the room's purpose was a studio. I could see nothing. I slapped the wall looking for a light switch, found none, and used a match. A naked bulb on a string hung from the ceiling. The light revealed a black cloth tacked to one wall. The kinds of light professionals used to illuminate indoor scenes sat on tripods and lined another wall. A bed filled the center of the room. The covers were thrown back; pillows dotted the edges of the mattress, and in the middle lay a damp red stain the size of a serving platter. Flies turned the stain nearly black. Connecting doors left and right joined the other offices. The left one stood open and the right one was closed.

I opened the door on the right and entered the third office. I pulled another string. In the weak light I saw a single bed with a chenille spread wadded at the foot of the mattress, a hot plate, and a pail that might have served as a sink, judging from the dirty dishes sitting in scum-crusted water. A chair and a small desk with two drawers hugged one wall. Papers lay scattered on the desk under a couple of pencils and a Bakelite phone. The plaster board walls were unpainted. Covering one wall were eight by ten glossies of women with impressive bare breasts in garter belts that held up black nylons. They also wore spiked heels and forced smiles, but nothing more unless you counted the hat on one of them. In some of the photos a man, always the same man, wearing boxer shorts and a hairy chest fondled or suggested, without actually showing, various sexual activities. The smiles on the women were lower wattage and more strained when the man was in the picture.

I picked up the phone, got a tone, and dialed Dotty Orland's number.

"Did Travis have a thin moustache and combed-back black hair with a widow's peak?" I asked when she answered.

"Yeah, but lots of men do," she answered. "What else you got?"

"A very hairy chest," I said, while pulling the bulb's string to get the light closer without turning it off. "Looks like a tattoo of an anchor on his left shoulder."

"That's him. He doesn't show that stuff to just anyone."

"He's not here to stop me and there's a good chance he won't be back."

She whistled. "You find the good stuff?"

"Pictures of women in underwear being mauled by Travis?"

"That's not the good stuff. Keep looking. I'll be there in twenty minutes."

"No, Dotty. This is a crime scene. Work out access with Woozy."

"Ace, Travis had the dirt on the whole town. If the cops, even your buddies, get their hands on it there's gonna be a shift in power. You and me, we can be trusted not to abuse it."

"I trust me, Dotty. If it's that rich can you resist temptation?"

"I've seen it and done nothing. Does that make me trustworthy?"

"You've seen it, but have you held it in your hands?"

"I could have bought some of it, but I didn't. Go ahead and ask me why I didn't and really piss me off."

"Okay, Dotty. Sorry. If it's that hot and either one of us starts flashing it around, we're smack in the cross-hairs."

"Been there before. So have you. See you in twenty."

With the office doors ajar, some of the stomach-turning stench seeped out of the office. The middle room was the worst, with its blood-soaked bed that had become home to the colony of flies. I found a filthy towel and started swatting. When the angry flies moved on, a better look confirmed a blood loss that would have exsanguinated the victim. I got the chenille spread from the other bed and threw it over the swamp and ran for open space. I managed not to gag, grabbed a gulp of what passed for fresh air, and made a tour of the three rooms.

By the time Dotty Orland got there, I was sure the "good stuff" was not at hand. Travis could have walled over a stash, but he wouldn't have had access without leaving a trail.

"Either he's not the vic and he took it with him," I said to her, "or he is and whoever killed him took it."

"Or we haven't looked in the right place," Dotty said. "He knew what he had, and he would have been careful."

"You're sure it's here?"

"I'm not sure of anything. Not even death and taxes. But where else would he have hidden it? We're not talking a real sophisticated guy. He was an opportunist who specialized in sin. He knew people wanted to take their clothes off and doing it in front of a camera wasn't a big leap."

"Why'd he tell you?"

"I was his sugar mama and got him the money he needed."

I spread my arms and said, "Couldn't have been much."

"Money wasn't his addiction. He got off on talking people into doing things they'd never done before. Especially women. He bragged he could talk any woman of any age out of her panties."

"Could he?"

"You mean me? Find the stash."

"Who's in there?"

"Can you be trusted with such juicy rumor?"

"Ha, ha, I deserve that."

"Yeah, you do, but I'm not saying. Let's find it and then we'll both know."

"Any ideas? Where was it when you saw it before?"

"He carried samples in an orange print box."

"Prints! He had to do his own developing so where's the darkroom?"

We couldn't see the far end of the warehouse through the fog which had gotten thicker as the day outside grew warmer. I'd already taken off my jacket, and as it became obvious we were about to take a walk, Dotty took off her light green cloth coat that came down to her knees. Under it she wore a dark green short sleeve dress. Her shoes could travel so we started walking. We had to weave around puddles as the dripping moisture found every uneven low spot in the floor. With a couple of hundred feet to go we could see there was nothing but open space all the way to the loading door. We used the people-sized door, and moved on to the next warehouse.

"Let me play detective, Dotty," I said, as I checked the hinges. "Nobody's been through here for a long time. Let's stay outside and go around and check the other door. Unless you want to give up."

"Keep walking, Ace," she said, and she turned toward the parking lot.

"Let's take the river side," I said. "Reduces the chance we'll be seen, and I can check the wharf."

We walked the planks that had held millions of tons of supplies. Rusty railroad tracks hogged the middle of the dock, and bare pilings that had held the cranes that swung nets full of goods into the holds of the ships, rotted at the wharf's edge. The machinery itself had been dismantled long ago and moved to still functioning ports. Every twenty yards I stooped over the edge and stared into the dark water with my fingers crossed that I didn't see anything like a body or a slick that might be blood. Dotty watched the warehouse side.

When we reached the end of the building, I checked the door hinges for rust and found it. The next building's hinges showed the same. We patrolled the wharf with me doing my twenty-yards-then-stare-into-the-water routine.

"I think the river's getting pretty high," Dotty said.

"Keep your eyes on your side."

"There's nothing to see," Dotty called. A few seconds later, she said, "Yes, there is. I got a door here."

The door had been an add-on to the original construction. It sat partially blocked between twin stacks of decaying pallets dressed up with torn tarpaulins. The door had a dead lock and a keyed knob. I tried keys from the ring in Travis' car, and got them open.

The rectangular room would have been pitch black had the door been closed. A two by four leaned inside the door. When it served its purpose no one could interrupt Travis. File cabinets with locks and wide shelves holding large, flat boxes lined the walls. In the middle was a three by six foot table under an overhead light. I unlocked the cabinets while Dotty found the light. A door in the short wall led to a large darkroom.

"He could develop a lot of prints in here," Dotty said, looking over my shoulder.

"Start an inventory, Dotty. I'll be outside."

I doubted Travis walked here from his studio each time he wanted to develop film. On the well-worn planks, I found marks where he'd turned his car around to pull it in between more stacks of pallets. To anyone not driving or walking the dock, he would be invisible. I looked closer and found a long piece of tarpaulin on rings through a rope. I pulled on the rope and the use made itself clear. It worked like a shower curtain to keep his car from being seen by river traffic. It was a lot of trouble unless he had something valuable to hide.

I found Dotty opening and closing file cabinet drawers. Folders jammed with paper and photographs filled each one. I reached around her for a folder in the middle.

"Hold it, Ace. Let's take a look and see what we've got before we start pulling stuff out. You know how organized I am."

She didn't take anything all the way out. Instead she browsed the tabs, peeled folders far enough back to see the edges of the contents, and worked her way to the bottom drawer. She finished her survey of the last file cabinet and brushed her hands on her skirt.

"First one is business stuff. Bills, a tax return, nothing too exciting. Second one is his 'if it bleeds let it lead' crap. Car wrecks, stuff he'd get chasing ambulances. I've seen a lot of it. Not much profit in it unless he got lucky. Then comes the celebrity stalking shots. I don't see a lot of organization. Maybe the order meant something to him, but we could be here all night."

"What else?"

"The last two hold his porn. First one's pretty tame. Mostly lingerie and suggestion. I doubt he'd go to jail unless he tried selling it on a school ground. The good stuff starts halfway through the third drawer and fills the last one. The tabs on the folders don't mean a thing to me. We're going to have to start our own system."

"How long to do it all?"

"Both of us? All night. Maybe more. I wasn't kidding."

"Okay. Let's lock up and go back to your office. We can get what we need to do the job right and get some food. We'll take a cab back. I don't want a car sitting around out there."

She looked at the file cabinet.

"Lot of misery in those drawers, and a lot of people know it."

"So how's he stayed alive this long?" I asked. "He had to have a plan to unleash all this woe, like if he disappears the flood gates open."

"Then why haven't they?" she asked.

"Maybe it hasn't been long enough," I said, pushing her toward the door. "Come on. We'd better plan for the worst, which means we don't have much time. How long since you've seen him?"

I locked up then we walked fast along the wharf.

"Probably a couple of weeks, but I only saw him when he had something to sell."

I almost missed it in the faint afternoon light. As we turned the corner from the dock to Travis's office, I saw smears on the planks that could be blood. I put my arm out and stopped Dotty.

I followed the blood to the edge of the dock. A rope hung from a stanchion and dipped into the river. I gave a tug. It didn't give. I sighed, and pulled harder with both hands. A leg with a man's shoe on its foot came out of the water. The rope was tied to the shin.

"Got a guess at how much Travis weighed?" I asked her.

"Maybe one-sixty. Why?"

"I'm going to have to pull harder. I'd say it's him down there."

I let go of the rope.

"Aren't you going to pull him out?" she asked.

"No. Now I am going to call the cops. How fast can you get back?"

"Half hour, but if the cops take the pictures – ."

"Then let's make sure they don't. Give me a ride to the gate."

She drove and I said, "I'll give you forty-five minutes to get back. Be sure to take a cab and bring a flashlight. I'll meet you at the gate."

She dropped me in the shadows and I watched her drive away. Across Front Street, a car turned its lights on. As it pulled onto Front, I saw two more cars parked nearby. Cigarette smoke came from one. I didn't know if they'd seen me, so I kept to the dark spots and cut over to the river side as soon as possible. It would have been more of a surprise if there had been no one watching the warehouse.

I stood on the dock and looked out into the black river. If Dotty was right about Travis having the whole town by the balls, how come he had lived like this? Getting his kicks by talking the town's bored housewives out of their clothes didn't explain it. Nobody would who didn't have to live in one room with a single bed, a hot plate, and a stinking pot to wash dishes in. Either Travis had somewhere else to call home, or he wasn't a blackmailer, and I couldn't imagine a motive for killing him if it didn't connect to him and his camera. If not for "the good stuff," maybe I could see a jealous husband or boyfriend, but the good stuff did exist, and hanging Travis in the river by a leg was no impulsive act of jealous rage.

I was sure a man had killed him. The body had been carried from the bed after it bled out, a rope tied to it, and then lowered over the side. A woman might have dragged the body to the edge, tied the rope around the leg, and kicked him over. If she had, either she was strong enough to tie a very good knot, or the impact with the water, with some help from the current, would have separated the rope from the body.

But why save the body at all unless it was meant to be retrieved? If that was the case, it definitely ruled out a woman. Travis' clothed, waterlogged body would weigh close to two hundred pounds. Maybe a woman could dead lift the weight, but why would she create a plan that called for it in the first place?

The day was late enough for Woozy to have finished his day shift. On day shift he went home after work, on swing it was Woo Fong Louie's, and on graveyard it was Giga's for breakfast. I looked around the dock and the warehouses, and thought it would be a good place to make a stand. I went inside and called him at home. He answered.

"You heard of a photographer named William Travis?" I asked.

"Muckraker and general pain in the ass."

"Yeah. He's dead and it's our business. Can you get Jesse?"

"Do I need him?"

"Tell him Terminal Four is a damn fine place to make a stand. You got anything to shoot with left in the Packard, or did you leave it all at my place?"

"We can still hold our own."

"Good. It's just in case. Turn right past the gate and watch for me."

"This had better be good. I already got my shoes off."

"It'll pay the rent for another few days, as someone recently told me."

Chapter 10

I saw the cab drop Dotty at the gate. The hack driver opened the trunk and stacked boxes on the ground. Dotty waved him off and stood still until he was gone. I scared her when she heard my running steps as I came to help. I scooped boxes and told her to get a move on. She wanted to know why, but I couldn't run and talk at the same time. I got the last box tucked out of sight of the gate and beat Woozy's Packard by less than a minute.

"That's why. The cops," I said. "Remember, nobody but me through the door. And stay inside, even if you hear shooting."

I had to run to catch the Packard. While I did, I looked to where the cars across the road had been earlier. I didn't see anything, but it was dark. Woozy used the spotlight mounted on the Packard's wing window. The spot on the other side was on, too, which meant he'd recruited Pugh. I caught the car and ran ahead waving my arms. They followed me to Travis's car. They got out and Woozy smoked while I caught my breath.

"Run's pretty good for a dead guy," Pugh said.

"Tell us why we got to give up an evening at home for a scumbag like Travis," Woozy said, as he crushed his smoke with a massive shoe.

They followed me to the dockside with its rope and dead weight end. I told them how I'd found Travis thanks to the photo of Melvin Jackson and Christina Bell that he'd taken at the Lullaby and he'd sold to Dotty Orland. I told them about going in and finding the flies and the porn, then checking outside.

"He's down there on that rope?" Woozy asked.

"How dumb is that?" Pugh asked. "Fish ain't going to leave much. Whoever dumped him shoulda let him drift off into the sunset where he can be someone else's problem. Let's take a look at the porn."

"Travis dead ain't the whole problem," I said. "Supposedly Travis had photos of prominent people more up front than usual."

"You find them?" Woozy asked. I shook my head.

"How up-front – like ready for action?" Pugh asked.

"The way I heard it he had the town by the balls."

Pugh and Woozy exchanged looks, then Woozy whined, "How come you know this and we don't?"

"That's not the real question. If he had all this power, what was he doing living here?"

"Ain't no figuring some people," Pugh said. He looked at the river and the crumbling dock. "You find those photos, Ace, you got the balls in your hand."

"That's why we're here," I said. "We've got some ethics."

"That would be us," Pugh said. "Let's take a look at the porn."

Despite Jesse's words, the porn came last. They took care of business one room at a time. Neither said much until Woozy lit another Chesterfield as we stood in the warehouse before entering the third room and its wall decorations.

"You take a look in this mausoleum while it was still light?" he asked, waving to the warehouse at large.

"Empty other than its own weather."

"How about the rest of them?"

"Looked in the next one and it was just as empty. Then I walked the wharf, found the rope, and called you."

He took two long drags.

"So what are you worried about? You think there's something here you haven't found?"

"How come Travis – if it is Travis – is still hanging in the drink like a big fish keeping fresh?"

"Sure as hell ain't fresh," Pugh said.

"Right, so what's the point?"

"Come on," Woozy said, "let's get him out of the river so we know what we got."

We all used flashlights and lit our own way back to the rope.

"Man, I hate floaters," Jesse said, putting down his light and reaching for the rope. He started pulling. "Feel free to chip in, y'all."

Woozy waved at me, and I got a grip on soggy rope. We kept pulling until the shoe, then the leg, cleared the planks.

"Shit!" Pugh yelled, "skin's falling off!"

I grabbed for the shin. My fingers tightened on pant leg until I felt bone, and I pulled.

"Goddamn," Jesse muttered, "I could have been a chef. If I had, the only dead meat I woulda touched woulda been pork ribs and brisket."

"How can you think about food?" I asked, as more decayed body came into sight.

"I can talk about food anytime, but this is still pretty fucking disgusting."

We had to lift the body to get it over the curb of the dock or the wood would have stripped what remained of the flesh.

"That him?" Woozy asked as we all shone our lights on the body.

"Probably," I said. "I've only seen pictures of him in his shorts."

"I know why they left him," Pugh said. "They got careless. They were dunking him trying to make him talk and they killed him. Dumb shits."

"Maybe he talked and they were done with him," Woozy said. "Guess we won't know if he did or not until we find what they wanted. Ace, you weren't just being a good citizen calling me and Pugh out here. What's up?"

"Let's get inside," I said.

"You worried about somebody seeing us?" Pugh asked, looking around.

"Maybe. Why risk it?" We walked into the warehouse. "We want to know who and what's driving the changes. Maybe it's as simple as a giant blackmail scheme, and our blackmailer has a plan for taking over the town. Travis had a reputation for talking women out of their clothes, but maybe he's got more than pictures of women. Men, too. What if the rumors are right about his stash? What if whoever finds it winds up with the power?"

I waved them into the third office and pulled the string on the overhead bulb.

"Jesus!" Jesse said. "What a dump. No way that guy had the grip on the whole town."

Woozy used his flashlight to examine the photos on the wall. Jesse followed behind.

"Kind of a letdown," Woozy said. "Nobody would have killed over this stuff."

"My thoughts exactly," I said. "I think he lived someplace else, and this was for show. Somebody on the same trail we're on sees this and leaves Travis alone."

Woozy used the connecting door to enter the studio.

"Can't believe anybody with any class would have stripped down here. You think he had another spot for his seductions?"

"I think he lived in one place, and used another to shoot his good stuff. And I think he had a third place – make it a fourth place, counting this – for his stash and a darkroom."

"So how come Mr. Brilliant's feeding the fish?" Pugh asked.

"Because he reached too high. It's one thing to extort a common citizen, and another to take on the real power."

"So why take on the power?" Pugh asked. "He was getting laid and making money. Woulda been enough for me!"

"I think he seduced the wrong person. They found his scheme and decided to take over."

"I don't buy it," Woozy said. "We been seeing changes happening for a lot longer than Travis has been dead."

"I'm going to take a look outside," Jesse said. "Ace tells us to bring some firepower, but here we're blind as bats."

Woozy and I watched him go.

"What if it was jockeying for position?" I said after Pugh closed the door behind him. "Maybe whoever, say it's Arnold Newman, found out but took it slow to find the goods. How long's it been since things started to heat up?"

"A couple of months I guess," Woozy said, "but it feels like forever."

"Okay, so Arnold Newman finds out what Travis is doing, plays it cool trying to work Travis for the goods, and either kills him before he gets what he wants, or gets the stuff and then kills him."

"Either way we don't know," Woozy said. "How'd you find this place?"

"Dotty Orland. She'd bought a print of a shot Travis took at the Lullaby of Christina and Melvin. I did some checking on the guy then came looking."

"Where'd you check?"

"What's with all the questions?"

"I'm still a cop," Woozy said, "and you're not. I'm tired of getting the news from you."

"You got your sources and I don't ask. Don't ask me about mine."

"You know what else pisses me off, Ace? How many of your confidential informants are women? I'll bet they all are. I'll bet you got Maxine helping you, and Dotty Orland, too. And Hildy, goddamn it!"

"So women don't know anything?"

"No, goddamn it! They don't talk to me!"

"You get what you need out of the men. Between the two of us we got it covered."

From the door, Jesse clicked his torch. "We got company. Across Front. Two car loads at least. Probably more."

Woozy and I turned off our lights. By the time we reached Pugh, Woozy had his trunk key ready. The fog from across the river had moved in on us. The cars seventy yards away were dim outlines.

"They making a move?" he asked.

"Nah. Just saw the lights of two more cars. Makes four so far."

Outside, we crouched beside the Packard. Like a good cop, Woozy had parked facing toward the street so we could get into the trunk without exposing ourselves.

"M-1's on the right, a BAR in the middle. The ammo box has some spare clips and a couple of grenades."

"What's in the crate?" Jesse asked.

"White para flares and a flare gun."

"You called this party, Ace," Jesse said. "What's the plan?"

"I'll take the BAR and the clips. I'll hit them coming through the gate. Only two ways in: the gate or go around. If they go around they got to come down the dock."

"Three ways," Woozy said "The river. Maybe that's why they been slow making a move waiting to get the troops in place."

"Before we open fire," I said, lifting the heavy BAR to my shoulder, "it would be nice to know if these are really the bad guys."

"Got any ideas?" Jesse asked. "Wanna check their dog tags at the gate?"

"Let's force their hand," I said, pointing behind me at the warehouse. "Let's open the big doors and drive the Packard in. If it's them, they'll know we're loading up."

I found the bolt in the floor holding the door in place, and lifted it with my foot.

"They better not shoot up my car," Woozy said, and wasted no time as he drove inside. We pushed the door closed behind it.

"Lights across the street!" Jesse called.

I grabbed the BAR.

"Keep your heads down," I said.

"I'll take the river side," Jesse called over his shoulder, "That's my left and you don't want to be on it, partner."

The cars across the street had their engines and lights on, but hadn't made a move. The lights were diffused circles in the thickening fog.

"I'm going to set-up by those drums," Woozy said, pointing.

"Not much to stop a bullet."

"I want to cover both of you. Let's hit 'em hard and walk away clean."

"Maybe I shouldn't have phoned," I said, looking first at him and then where Jesse had gone to ground.

"We knew it was coming," he said, looking around. "Good a spot as any."

Still no movement across the street.

"What happens when you die?" he asked me.

"Nothing," I said.

"You telling the truth this time?"

"I got shot at the Lullaby. The next thing I remember was you calling me about Melvin."

"You don't remember coming back to life in the morgue, or me being at the hospital?"

"That's your memory, not mine," I said.

Engines revved.

"I might get my head blown off in the next minute. Come on, Ace, give me something!"

"What for Christ's sake?"

Woozy ran a hand through his hair and shook his head.

"What the fuck am I doing here?" he mumbled. "What are you doing here? Why do this?"

I thought about it and found only, "Adrenaline."

"That's it? The need to get blown away? The chance to get blown away? That's all there is?"

"As far as I know that's it. Uh-oh. Here they come."

"Ace! That all there is?"

"If you gotta go, embrace it."

"Welcome death? That's your advice?"

I stopped and thought of something.

"What's left undone?"

"Undone?"

"Yeah. If you see the bullet coming what's your last thought? It better not be I wished I hadn't left something undone."

"Dying with a clear conscience?"

"Yeah." I said, pointing at him. "Dying with no regrets."

"Beyond not wanting to die? I'm good, I guess."

"Good. Now get out there! Give 'em a helluva fight."

Four cars came abreast across the street and faced us.

"Spend a flare when they hit the gate," I called toward Woozy as we ran. I found a spot on the pavement that gave me a wide field of fire, kicked the front legs of the automatic rifle into place, and lay down behind it. I had no cover but no one would be shooting back if I did my job. The 30-06 rounds from the automatic would shred the thin tin of the jalopy's body and occupy the shooters' minds right before it opened their heads like melons. I hadn't used a BAR since the war, but it felt like yesterday as I stacked two spare clips where I could grab them.

The row of cars broke apart. Two came toward the gate. Two more headed for the fence intending to create their own way in.

Woozy fired a flare as two cars came through the gate side by side. The light became defused with the fog but did little to improve visibility. I hadn't seen fog like this since the Bulge when warmer weather turned the frozen ground to an impenetrable vapor.

I hesitated because I still doubted their intentions, but gunfire toward Woozy settled the issue. I aimed at the passenger sides slightly above the engine because I wanted to give the drivers a chance to swerve to give me a broadside shot. I used short bursts into each. As the bullets ripped through their metal bodies, the cars' engine compartments started spewing steam. I saw the windshields disintegrate. The car on my right tried to turn too hard too fast and rolled onto its side. I slammed more rounds into the exposed roof, no longer caring who I hit.

Something hit the pause button in my head. My world went still lying on the ground behind the rifle on the docks in the rain with steam coming off the barrel. Out of the fog came a replay from another life where I lay not on concrete but in the mud of a road in Belgium. I lay behind another BAR, and bandolier after bandolier of ammo linked together for continuous fire. I was the roadblock to keep a convoy of Krauts away. If the Germans got by me my buddies would die.

The familiar howl of Nazi half-tracks, a higher pitch than the dreaded growling of the tanks, rolled out of the fog. Seconds later came the vehicles and beside them foot soldiers. I fired. The big armor-piercing rounds from the BAR ripped into the radiators of the trucks; engines blew, men fired back. I pressed deeper into the slush of the melting snow and trusted the flash suppressor and the fog to keep the enemy from getting a fix on me. I backed off the trigger and picked my targets, swiveling the barrel across the field of fire. Every second I held them, more of my comrades would cross the river. That was the whole point of me lying here.

There was no one holding a seat on the boat for me and I knew it.

The present came to life.

The other car, the one I hadn't blown to dust, wobbled as it made its turn but held its tires. It lost speed and its engine quit. Shooters inside returned fire, some of it for me and the rest for Woozy. By now he had one of the cars that had crashed the fence weaving toward him. I riddled my target, the second car through the gate, left exposed in the open. I poured round after round into it until the belt went dry. I changed to the next one and shifted targets to the fence buster. Bullets from both Woozy and me thumped into the car. With the first impacts, side doors came open. Woozy tossed a grenade. An explosion rocked the car then flames lit the night. In the light of the fire engulfing the car, I saw one of the escaped shooters fling his arms in the air. Shrapnel, I thought, and reloaded again.

I looked up, and not a creature stirred from the car on its side. I lifted the BAR, and ran in a crouch toward a spot where I could be more use to Woozy. I didn't see the second car that had knocked the fence down. They must have doused their lights when they saw their buddies getting lit up. If they were smart they got out of the car.

Shots came whizzing by me and I went sprawling. The bad thing about the BAR if you have to shoot from a prone position is that you need to drop the bi-pod legs first. I had no target, but I dumped twenty rounds in the general direction of the shots.

While I'd moved, strategically, our position had worsened. Woozy had taken fire, and I couldn't tell what trouble Jesse faced. Maybe he'd been lucky. We'd only seen four cars and we'd accounted for three. There was some light from the burning car but it didn't help spot our targets. I waited for Woozy to fire another flare. He didn't.

"Woozy," I yelled. "I'm covered. Light one up!"

He must have been holding the flare gun. The sudden light caught two men making a run toward the river. Woozy and I took them down.

With the flare lighting the area, all I had going was a low profile. Shots from the shadows pinged off the ground nearby. I didn't see any muzzle flashes, but I took a chance and fired. I saw Woozy move as my covering fire held the shooters down. He made a wide end run using what cover he could find. Shots came my way again. My face stung from ricochets kicking debris. I covered my face, and wished Woozy a quick journey and good aim. Two shots impacted the warehouse wall just over my head as the shooters found their range.

With the blink of my twisted existence, the ground under me turned back to mud. I was back in Belgium face down in the mud. Bullets struck all around me. Geysers of mud splashed my face; something hot burst into my arm. The enemy came closer. Still the BAR chattered and I saw men die. So many had gone down the ones behind had to climb over them to get closer.

The BAR went dry.

I exploded into a world of pain. As I screamed at my failure to protect those who trusted me, a light inside me absorbed me and I became it. Later, I would think of that as the moment I died.

Back on the docks, the soft scent of honeysuckle, like a veil floating on a breeze, captured my roving senses. I lay again on the rain-soaked paving on the docks of Island City.

Woozy's last flare died. The shooters held their fire. Darkness and deeper shadows, a different version of the black on black I'd experienced in the crane closed around me. A sigh -- no discernable word, just a deep breath -- whispered in my ear. I thought of a lover with her mouth over my ear. The sensation strengthened and became more substantial than my last visit from the woman in black. The greater definition intensified my sense of dread. I knew I was no longer part of the battle around me. Nor was I blown up in the Bulge.

"What are you?" I whispered into the void between worlds. The void did not frighten me. There was a familiar-ness to it that welcomed me.

The whisper on the breeze came again. This time long enough for me to recognize a bar from the song I sang to the woman in black in the crane.

"Are you luck?"

"Uhoooo," said the sound in my ear. More a 'no' than a 'yes. '

"Are you a lady?"

"Ssssss." I counted that a yes.

"Are you death?"

"What is the real mystery, Danny?"

The voice faded, and the scent changed from honeysuckle to cordite and fear.

The visitation, now gone, had lasted no more than seconds. The moment ended with an explosion from the dock. Light flooded the area where our attackers were held up. Woozy and I fired even though we had no target. I emptied a clip chewing up what I hoped was poor cover for the shooters. I waited. Nothing.

Woozy came out of his cover in a crouch.

"Check Pugh," he called. "I'll make sure these guys are goners."

I ran to the corner. A fire burned in the old wood decking. Behind me I heard two single shots. Woozy closed accounts as he walked.

I saw the silhouette of a man on the ground in front of the flames. I ran to him. Jesse lay with his eyes open looking at me.

"Will I be back like you, Ace?"

"Let it be, Jesse," I said, and took his hand. I squeezed and he returned it. I heard pounding feet coming from behind me. "Feel the peace."

"Ah, shit! Jesse!" Woozy said, dropping to a knee and knocking me aside. "What happened?"

"A boat. Incendiary grenade. Didn't hear no shot. Just the boom. Partner, Ace says it's good to die. Am I coming back like him?"

"Don't worry about it, Jesse," Woozy said. "You ain't going to die."

"Bullshit to both of you. Already dead from the brain down."

Woozy looked at me. I saw tears in his eyes. "Give the man his answer."

"Jesse," I said.

"Ace!" Woozy barked.

"Sure, Jes – " Jesse Pugh's eyes glazed and I saw the promise of death, a black hole with a silver lining glowing in the gloom, engulf him. "Sure Jesse, you'll be back and me and Woozy will be here waiting for you."

Woozy closed Jesse's eyes and stood. "You couldn't just lie and tell him what he wanted to hear."

"I told him what he needed to hear!"

Would Jesse Pugh be my moment of failure that would send me back to Island City again because I failed to hold his hand into the next world?

"*Nooooo*," came the whisper in my ear.

Woozy stood and slowly reloaded his revolver. The deliberateness of it sent a message of death as strong and violent as any I'd seen this day.

"Find me a survivor," he said, and took my arm. "One will do."

"They're shot up pretty bad," I said.

"Move it, Ace! He won't need to live long."

I walked into the devastation caused by our well-aimed weapons. Minutes before, the cars lying twisted and mangled had been functional autos containing human beings. Now they were shot-up wrecks holding dead bodies covered in blood. There were no survivors. A few had survived until Woozy's last tour of the killing grounds. Now they lay sprawled in the way only death discards the living.

"Well?" Woozy asked as he walked up.

"Nothing."

He reached into the car and jerked a dead face around to the light. He did the same thing with two more bodies then leaned back.

"The cops are going to be hiring," he said. "I recognize all three of them. This one's named Slocum. That one's Pitarelli, and the last guy's Farmer or Francis. Something like that."

I followed Woozy as he inspected the other bodies. He took badges out of every pocket. He looked into his massive hands that cupped his collection. He leaned his head back and howled into the fog. The misery in his voice became the echo of the battle on the wharf.

I don't know how long the shootout had lasted, but hundreds of rounds had been fired, at least two grenades had exploded, flares had lit both the night and the dock fire, and two cars had been burned. Not a siren to be heard. It was as if this were a Pacific atoll or maybe a mountain pass in Italy where battles of noise and carnage went on for days.

"What do you want to do?" I asked Woozy.

"Let's get Jesse in the Packard. I want you to go with me to take him to the hospital and file the report. Adele's going to get her widow's pension. Every fucking dime. Don't forget to reload."

Before we left, we pulled the three bodies Woozy identified and pulled a tarp over them. An hour later Jesse lay in the morgue properly named and respected.

"Do lions have dens?" Woozy asked, as we left.

"Yeah, sure. You know the expression 'beard a lion in his den?'"

"Then let's beard ourselves some lions."

I covered Woozy's back as we went in the front door of Central Precinct. None of the cop's eyes sitting in the half-empty detective's room met ours, but that might have been because of the way we looked. Dirt and grime and blood streaked our shirts and slacks and faces. We walked the walk of the survivor, the walk of men who were cocked and loaded for more. We both carried .45's at our sides, and back up pieces in plain sight. Woozy pushed through the swing gate and stared at the desks. He walked to a desk where a shiny new name plate read *Jack Slocum*. He picked it up, inspected it, and slammed it in the waste can. He did the same at the desks with plates that read Pitarelli and Franks. He showed me the last one and shrugged before he dropped it in the can. Then he finished his tour checking name tags against badges tossing the latter on the desk and the former in the waste cans. In all eight echoes of tin garbage cans thundered through the silent room, each crash marking the death of a cop dead in the pursuit of evil.

We didn't knock at the door to the watch commander's office. A cop I didn't recognize wearing captain's bars spluttered and started to stand up.

"Get out of here and arrest Spader before I have you tossed in the can!"

The plate on his desk said his name was Marsh. Woozy took him by the hair, pulled his head back, and fit his gun under the man's jaw line.

"Pugh is dead," Woozy said, and shoved the end of his gun harder into Marsh's neck. "So are the pitiful morons you sent to kill us. The ones in the boat made it – so far. You will approve a "Killed in the Line of Duty" for Pugh. I want his wife to get every penny she deserves."

"I can't do it," Marsh said. "He wasn't on duty."

Woozy thumbed the hammer back.

"Do it or die."

"Fuck you. You're as good as dead, too."

Woozy shifted the barrel to the right.

"What difference does it make?" Marsh yelled. "We're all going to die anyway. The floods are coming and everyone will

ACE HIGH by Ken Byers

drown. Just like last time. The whole fucking town will disappear! Maybe it will happen again, and again, and again! None of this matters, you crazy bastard!"

Woozy pulled the trigger. Part of Marsh's ear disappeared in a red mist.

"Maybe you can kill me, but what about Ace here?" Woozy yelled into Marsh's other ear. "You can't kill him. He doesn't die!"

Marsh still looked defiant through the shock of half his ear being blown off.

"Don't you get it? None of this is real!" Marsh yelled through his pain.

"How many times you died, Ace?" Woozy screamed so Marsh would hear. I shrugged. "You ever going to stop until the score's even?"

Marsh stared, fear replacing pain.

Woozy let go of Marsh and picked up his name plate. He wiggled it over the waste can, the question clear.

Marsh's eyes locked on Woozy. "Fuck you. I hate drowning."

Woozy used all his bulk to throw Marsh back into his desk chair which went over backward sending him sprawling. He stood over him, took careful aim, and pulled the trigger.

We walked slowly through the squad room again, guns hanging in our hands. No one moved. Hands stayed where we could see them.

"Goddamn it!" Woozy yelled pointing the barrel from one man to the next. Some ducked under their desks. Some closed their eyes and sat with their lips moving. "Somebody try something. I want more blood!"

Not a muscle twitched.

As I held the door for him, Woozy yelled, "Fuck!" and then fired a round into the ceiling.

Outside, we stood next to the Packard.

"Can you get back on your own?" Woozy asked. "I got to make sure my wife's okay, and then pick up Adele. I can get them some place safe so Trixie can help Adele."

"You want the crane?"

"That shit hole? It's okay for you, but not for them. You going back there?"

"No. Terminal Four. Travis's cameras are still there. I want to get some shots of our corpses. You never know. Let's leave messages for each other at Giga's. We can count on Pearl." Woozy opened the car's front door, but before he got in, I asked, "Hey, what happened to my name-plate?"

"I don't know. It was on my desk for a while. People started asking what the 'T' stood for and how come there was no last name."

"What did you tell them?"

"The name was too long. Besides, the guy who did the plates couldn't spell it."

"Why didn't you just tell them no one knows?"

"Makes you less than real, my friend."

I put my hand on his massive shoulder. "Am I your friend?"

"Fuck, I don't know nothin'. You killed and protected at my side. I'll settle for whatever that makes you. See ya."

When I reached Terminal Four, nothing had changed. Bodies still cooled inside the burned-out wrecks of the cars, the three corpses Woozy and I moved were still where we'd left them, and the dock still glowed from the fire. I stood at the river's edge in the spot where Jesse Pugh died, and sniffed the air. No hint of honeysuckle, but a chill gripped my spine. What was I really doing here?

Who was I?

What was the meaning of life, or more to the point, the meaning of death?

I dredged up a memory that said in order to have lived a good life, each man had to find some meaning for his actions. Maybe here the inverse was true. In order to die a man had to find some meaning in his death. The honeysuckle had become the prompt to hold onto these thoughts and find understanding. The chill deepened and my head hurt. The idea was like an echo.

I had stood here before; had the same thought before. No idea when, as if time mattered. I was sure it was since the Bulge but before this.

A thud against the dock jerked my attention. Before I let go, I closed my eyes and offered to let the shadow flitting inside my mind lead me to understanding. It declined. No flight of fancy or fantasy swept me into a better elsewhere.

I sighed and accepted my busted fate. I looked over the edge of the dock and into the river. More debris filled the river as the water level climbed up the piling. The embers from the smoldering dock behind me twinkled across the water. Where the sparkling red ripples stopped, so did what I could see.

Might as well be the edge of existence.

Chapter 11

I went looking for Dotty. I wondered what she'd thought during the war outside her shell, or even if she was still barricaded behind the door.

"Dotty! It's Ace!"

After a few seconds, the door opened. She'd turned the light off and I heard her before I saw her.

"You'd better be alone. I've got a gun," she said with an intensity that left no room for doubt.

"It's just me."

"Come in. Lock the door behind you." Her voice moved slowly around the room. I visualized her circling the table in the middle. "Okay, now lock it."

"Easier if I could see."

"Remember those words. Just do it my way."

"What if you aren't alone?"

"I'm alone. All goddamn night while it sounded like the world went to hell!"

I secured the door and she turned the light on. It took a few seconds for my eyes to adjust. We squinted at each other across the table covered with scattered piles of photos.

"You fight Iwo Jima again out there?" she asked, eyes wide. "What the hell happened?"

"Men died. They were cops sent to take out me, Woozy, and Jesse Pugh. Jesse didn't make it. Neither did the cops. Dotty, ever notice how often we refer to the war? You said it sounded like Iwo out there."

"For Christ's sake! It did."

"How long ago was it? Iwo, I mean."

"Feels like yesterday."

"Yesterday, eh? What do you remember most about it?"

"What's that got to with this?" she asked, pointing at the table.

"Humor me."

She made it clear she didn't want to before she finally gave in.

"Remember most? Like the clearest?"

"Come on, Dotty. What do you remember?"

Her eyes glazed and slowly climbed to somewhere beyond my right shoulder. I knew nothing lurked behind me but darkness.

"I always thought I'd have time to make my life count."

"That's it?"

"You never thought about it?" Her eyes came back to mine.

"I'm still thinking about it! Why did you think it then?"

I watched the memory absorb her. Her face filled with fear, and her arm came up extended to fight the memory off.

"I was always afraid of fire," she said.

"Me, too."

"The casualties were so bad. Oh, Ace, it breaks my heart to let the memories in! Life after life dying right in front of me." Tears rolled from her eyes. "We'd moved the intake station closer to the action. It was a tough decision, but Marines were dying on the way to us, so we went to them. Even though it was more dangerous, none of the medical crew held back. We were there for a purpose and our lives meant no more than anyone else's. Were you there?"

"No, Europe. I was at the Bulge. I don't remember where I was during Iwo."

"War is chaos," she said. "Small groups surviving any way they can."

She stopped. Her face said she was getting to the worst of it.

"Our guys were using flamethrowers to drive the Japs out of their tunnels. Just like we had trouble getting the wounded off the line, it was hard getting replacement tanks to the flamethrower teams. I saw the new tanks stacked near our station."

She dropped her hand and I saw the memory suck her in.

"That's how bad it was. Death everywhere, lurking every place, and we set up to save lives next to something like that. A mortar shell must have set them off. The air got pulled out of my lungs right before the light. That's when I knew I'd never make my life count."

"Then what happened?"

"What scares me, Ace, is maybe I'm dead. Right now."

"That makes me a figment of your death."

"You ever see the light? Not a light across a room, but a light that comes on inside you, and makes you part of it. You ever see that light?"

I didn't tell her about the BAR going dry.

"We're more important than figments of each other's death," I said. "Besides, when Iwo happened you were a nurse. You lived because you came out of the war a correspondent."

"How do you know?"

"You told me. Why else would you be doing what you're doing?"

"The cutting service? Maybe I can't find a better place to look for the secret of life. Maybe I'm a nurse saving lives a whole different way! In these," she pointed at the photos on the table, "people are having sex in all shapes and sizes and not one happy face. This is not the sex of orgasms. This is the sex of humiliation and degradation. Like mortal wounds from something other than guns and bombs and exploding tanks of napalm. That the way you want to feel now?"

"Get laid or die? No, but then my picture isn't in that stack."

"You sure? Maxine's is in there."

A lump settled in my stomach, then dissolved.

"I'd be surprised if she wasn't. Isn't that what she does?"

"I've seen her at Frills. She looks like she's having fun. In there," she tapped the stack with a fingernail, "she looks like she's trapped in Dante's second circle of Hell."

"Which one is that?"

"Lust. You in love with her?"

I thought about it. "I wish I could say yes, but it's not love."

"What is love to you?" she asked. "Thinking about someone and being happy when you do?"

"No, it's more than that."

"Like what?"

"Love fills me up. There's no room for anything else."

"You ever love like that?" Dotty asked.

I looked up into my own darkness and sorted my senses.

"My head says no, but the rest of me says yes. How could I know that if I hadn't done it?"

She pulled the photos out of my reach.

"What are you doing?" I asked.

"You special man," she said, reaching a hand for my face. "You can't see these pictures. They would destroy you."

"Oh, come on. I can take porn."

She walked around the table reaching for me. When I came close enough she took my hand.

"Ace, this world can't afford to lose your view of love. This," she tapped the overturned photos, "isn't porn. Calling something porn is more a statement on society. This is the defacing of each person who's in there. You with me? Our most intense human experience depicted as futile and ugly. You look at this and you'll never want to make love, or never allow a partnership that produces a child. This," she tapped harder, "is the end."

"Come on, Dotty, you're making Travis sound like evil personified."

"Maybe. At least he held the camera." I reached for the photos, but she put her hand on mine and shook her head. "Ask yourself what's going on here. We are in a room inside a room – a world inside a world – maybe a life inside a life."

"You're scaring me."

"Good. In the last couple of minutes we've touched on the meaning of life, the nature of death, marriage, what love is, and, oh yeah, sex. Most couples go a lifetime without talking about any of them. Don't tell me this is just another day on the job."

She stood against the table looking at me. When I didn't say anything, she went on.

"You ever want to take a boat to the other side?" she asked.

"The other side of what?"

"The river!" she yelled, her frustration showing. "Rivers have bridges and boats that go back and forth, but not us and no one seems to mind or even notice. That river should have been named Acheron instead of North."

"You saying this is Hell?" I asked.

"All that's missing is the sign."

"Bullshit. This ain't hell."

"How about purgatory then?" She took a turn looking at the ceiling maybe hoping to find the kind of insight I found. "I'm on a journey looking for the meaning to a life I was sure I'd lost. Now, talking to you, I know I lost that life and I'm trapped in some kind of purgatorial loop."

"A what?"

"This is purgatory!" she yelled. "You ever go to church?"

"I don't think so."

"This is like the waiting room. Not alive and not dead. We got sidetracked on our way to eternity. Maybe we did something wrong, or didn't do something we were supposed to. You know, left something undone."

I thought about what I'd told Pugh. Now, I had no idea where those words had come from. Maybe I was supposed to tell Jesse and then forget them.

She warmed to her subject and her eyes took on a new light.

"Maybe this," she meant the world around us not this room, "is where you hang out if there's a chance for redemption. You keep getting a shot to do it again and get it right. If you do, you get the highball to Heaven. You don't, you do it again."

I looked at her in the weak light of the darkroom where the photos depicting the failure of the human condition had been developed, and contemplated her vision of purgatory.

"Maybe there's a bunch of waiting rooms," I said. "If there are then this is the purgatory where people who died in the war before they finished their mission go."

"You gotta think more exclusive than that, Dan T."

"Okay, how about people who died trying to do the right thing but they got a lot of past sins chasing them along. This is the place you work out which way you're going."

"So if they hadn't died trying to do right," she said, "they'd be in Hell."

"But because they did, they get a do-over."

She nodded and contemplated my words.

"I'd been wondering why I met you," she said. "You're this idealistic knight jousting at windmills with bad guys trying to kill you, but you're hell-bent on finding your way out. I wonder what happens if you find your way and I don't."

"I'm gone. You're not."

"What makes you think so?"

"People disappear around here all the time. They found their answer."

"Or ran out of do-overs," she said.

I stared at her.

"That's it!" The answer lit up in my head like neon. "You gotta be willing to live and die on your record."

"You mean, don't go around whining you want to come back."

"Right! You play the cards you hold," I said, pointing at her, "and hope it's good enough to get that highball sign."

"How you doing on that?" she asked.

"Hell, I don't even know what I'm supposed to be doing!"

"No clues?"

"No, I got clues. Delinda Paz. She says I'm making progress from the times I've been here before. She says she's hopeful."

"Who the hell is she, I mean beyond a gossip collector?" Dotty asked.

"Let me throw this wrinkle at you," I said. "What if the power players have all changed? What if all the power sits with the women?"

"Long overdue if it's true," Dotty said, "but nothing in my life says you're right."

"I got three nominees," I said, raising a hand and preparing to tick the three off my fingers. "Delinda, Hildy, and in third place, Max."

She shook her head.

"I don't like it. That just calls in the fog again. It was clean when us soldiers who died trying to fight the good fight were still trying. Add the women and now where are we?"

I shrugged.

"I don't know, Dotty. I like simple, too, but it's not enough. I can't explain Island City without more players. We have to decide where to start."

"We have to decide if we're dead," she said.

I thought of the light that made me its own.

"I don't think it matters," I said. "We're here and we're on a mission. Our perceptions are all keyed to this place. So are our mysteries."

"Where do we start?" she asked.

"You said whoever had these pictures controls the town. Why, if it's not about sex?"

"It's much worse than sex. These are pictures of people having their souls stolen."

"That's it. These pictures are the losers, the ones who've run out of do-overs. Did you recognize anyone other than Max?"

"No, and I wonder about Maxine," she said. "The faces were blurry like they moved the instant the shutter opened."

"Or they were taken the instant their souls were yanked out of their bodies." I knocked the table top with a fist. "Let's get out of here and do something. This theorizing is making me crazy."

"Where you going to start?" she asked.

"I'm going to see me a pair of kings," said Ace Spader.

Chapter 12

A cross town trolley dropped me four blocks from my destination. I slowly walked those blocks through the Spew looking through the lens of my new assumptions. What had been the sticks and stones of a real world, I now saw as a manifestation of images pulled from the depths of my brain to create images of Dotty's purgatory. It looked disturbingly familiar. At a glance, nothing looked out of place or superficial. Closer inspection found storefronts without backs and people who all looked way too much the same. Maybe once you start to doubt, the brain doesn't try as hard. Maybe it isn't the brain at all.

I went through the same rigmarole as last time before ending up in the same chair across the desk from Birdlegs. He poured from the same bottle with a black label.

"Ace, my man, what brings you to my part of town?"

"How long you been here, Birdlegs?" I asked.

"Since the war, as if it was any of your business."

"Oh, it's my business. What you do in the war?"

"Not get killed."

"You sure about that?"

"I'm here, ain't I?"

"Let's come back to that. Any close calls?"

"One or two."

"Tell me."

"Don't like thinking about it."

"But you'll tell me."

His eyes went over my head like Dotty's had. I recognized it now; was even ready for it. It was like looking down a tunnel to the moment it would all end in a flash of light.

"I wasn't always like this," he said, and as he did his voice changed to a deeper baritone that fit the rest of him. "You want the story? Here it is. You know what a ball turret is?"

"You were a ball turret gunner?"

"Yeah, 24's out of Africa. You know what the mortality rate on ball turret gunners was?"

I shook my head, but I knew it was high. It was high for anyone who flew B-24 Liberators, but a lot of guys in that glass ball on the plane's belly died while the plane and other members of the crew lived to fly another day.

"There was a poem about the bodies of ball turret gunners getting washed out with a hose."

"That happen to you?" I asked.

He spread his arms indicating he sat in front of me, then his words belied the motion. "I wonder."

"What?"

"Now listen, Ace, don't you go thinking this really happened. This is more the nightmare you have too often that keeps you awake on bad nights. You have any of those?" He nodded toward the spot where I'd lain on the floor and supposedly died. "Anyway, I'm riding the belly ball. We climb up out of Libya toward the end of the line of 177 Liberators on that Operation Tidal Wave mission. Took a long time to launch that many bombers. August 1, 1943. Headed for Romania and all that German oil near Ploiesti. By the time we got within a hundred miles of our target the sky was black with burning oil fields, and 24's were dropping like stones. And a few Messerschmitts, too.

"You know the job of the belly ball-gunner?"

"It's the hole in the bottom so you can see what's coming at you from below."

"And shoot it down, or stop them from shooting you down. You got a pair of .50 mils and that's it. No chute because you ain't got room. You looking down 20,000 feet to the ground with nothing more than Plexiglas and a harness keeping you from the plunge."

"What happened that day?" I asked.

"Fifty-three of the Liberators didn't make it back. Don't know how many of the others made it back but weren't in one piece. That was us. My fault, too."

"How come?"

"One of the .50's jammed. Usually pretty reliable. One would shoot if the other was jammed, but I lost my cool, Ace. I tried to work the feed free on the one that jammed. I stopped shooting at the two fighters carving us out of the pack. Soon as I did, they closed. Probably figured I'd taken a hit. If I'd kept shooting, even with only one gun, it would have held them off. We took hits all down the fuselage. The fighters moved on with so many planes to shoot at. I don't know how, but the pilot -- don't remember his name -- got us across the water. Landing was bad. Undercarriage pretty shot up. Couldn't retract the ball turret – me – so I was just sort of hanging there. Can't tell you how I walked out of that. We landed, there was a huge flash of light, and pretty soon I'm walking away. Me and one other guy. And then," he managed a nervous chuckle, "I came here to become a pillar of the community."

"You remember much between the light and Island City?"

"Not much. Don't want to."

"What's it like here?" I asked. From his expression it was clear he'd never thought about it. "You just keep on keeping on?"

"Ain't bad. Set my own hours."

"What do you think would happen if you and the Judge disappeared?"

He laughed. "Never find out."

"Humor me. What do you and the Judge do for Island City?"

"Like I said, we the pillars of the community."

"Without you it would all go to hell," I finished for him.

He pointed at me and winked. I sat there so long without saying anything Birdlegs said, "You gonna leave, Ace, or just sit there?"

I still sat there trying to find a way to explain what he did in the context of Dotty's and my view of Island City.

"Sometimes there isn't an explanation," he said. "Sometimes all you get is a chance to keep going. You know? The pillars?"

I stood and walked out without a word.

Behind me Birdlegs called, "Just keep shooting, Ace!"

I crossed the half empty bar ignoring the bartender and pushed through the swinging doors to a landing at the head of the stairs that led down a full flight to the street. A naked bulb burned from the ceiling. At the bottom of the stairs I saw rain-soaked pavement reflecting the neon signs on the front of the building.

A third of the way down the steps the light changed. It all went dim. Not dark, but like half the wattage went elsewhere. I reached under my coat for the .45 in my waistband. By the time I had it out, two men with guns pointed up the stairwell at me and blocked the bottom. I ran down the stairs. I think I flew. I pulled the trigger. And pulled again until I emptied the gun at them. They got shots off, too, but I felt nothing. They weren't so lucky, if luck was what it was. They both took hits that spun and threw them to the ground. When I reached them the rain had already made rivulets from the blood draining out of them. When the stream reached the curb it fell into the steady flow from the quickening rain. Nobody stopped to look.

Up the street a purple Packard eased to a stop. I walked toward it. The passenger side door opened. I climbed in.

"No reason for me to get involved," Woozy said, and pulled into the flow of other vehicles. "What's next?"

"The Envoy," I said.

Woozy dropped me five blocks from the Envoy. I walked in the rain and looked around. Lights were on in second floor offices and businesses as Island City readied for flood stage. Outside the Virginia Café men lined up for sand-bags, and inside the owner's sons filled new ones like steam engines.

The Envoy stood alone as the luxury hotel in Island City. Most of the guests stayed longer than a week but no one made it a permanent address. The Envoy catered to the Calder Hills crowd who didn't want to or, for one reason or another, couldn't make the drive home. It wasn't as exclusive as the Athletic Club, but the clientele overlapped. No membership was required. They would rent me a room if I walked in with a bag and forked over more cash for one night than I spent on a month's rent at my flop. I doubted I would sleep any better in their beds.

From down the street hiding in my usual doorway, I used my monocular to scan the faces at the front door. The Judge's goons still stood around leaning on the facade and smoking. A cab stopped and unloaded a couple, with the man in a suit and the woman with a stole around her neck. The goons straightened up and palmed their smokes. They could lurk, but they weren't to scare the guests.

I made my way around the corner and found a booth. I called the Envoy and asked for Judge Ulysses Bell. They connected me without question. A voice I didn't know answered the phone.

"Who's calling?" it asked.

"Tell him his man in the middle."

"Who?"

"Give him the message."

A couple of minutes later the Judge came on the line.

"Spader?"

"Reporting in."

"Why? What could you possibly have to say?"

"Where's Hildy?"

The question caught him by surprise.

"With you?" he asked.

"You know she's not."

"I don't know where she is," he said.

"Are she and Christina together?"

"I thought I was paying you to know things like that."

"You're behind on the payments."

A long wait ticked by, then he said, "How long will it take you to get here?"

"Not long."

"Back door off the ally. I'll have a man there. Take the elevator to the roof."

The elevator came up a floor short, but I found the stairs. The door at the top sat blocked open.

"You and me, Spader," the Judge said. "No potato salad this time."

"Where were you in the war?" I asked him. I'd asked everyone else, so why not the Judge?

He looked slimmer, less substantial, in the short time since I'd seen him last. The lines in his face added years and his shoulders drooped.

"This is relevant how?"

"Humor me."

A smile creased his face that usually showed as little as a stone wall. He looked over the roofs of Island City and let the rain wash over his hatless head.

"London. Eisenhower's staff. Judge Advocate General's office."

"During the blitz?"

"Three years. Life here is easier."

"Any close calls?"

"Is this your morbid curiosity, or are we accomplishing anything I will be interested in?"

"Any close calls?"

"Several. The last one the air raid sirens caught me on the way home and I nipped down an entrance to the Tube. There were hundreds of us in the shelter. It flooded. I was one of the few who got out."

"You remember it like it was yesterday?"

He stood straighter and leaned toward me, his eyes scanning my face.

"I never gave it much thought."

"Why?"

"The way I saw it the shock of life erased the horror. Isn't that the way it is for most people? You? What do you remember when you got shot here?"

"I didn't die. It wasn't the first time I should have and didn't."

"Should or could?"

"Should. I've seen people die with less."

The Judge took his time answering, passing the time staring intently into the night that as far as I could tell hadn't changed a bit.

"What's this about?" he asked. "All the lucky ones who walked out of that war talk about close calls."

"How many lucky ones you know, Bell? I mean beside me and Birdlegs?"

He transferred his intent stare to me and tried to read my face behind the cascading water that failed to bother me.

"Is it possible, Dan T, that you're getting it?"

"Getting what?"

He waved at the night and the town below slowly taking on water.

"Island City! The why of it all."

"Tell me."

"If I do you'll be back. Is that what you want?"

"I already fucked it up. Jesse Pugh died. I shoulda saved him."

"That's it?" The Judge laughed. "Not even close. Guess I was wrong."

My turn to look at the night. I realized something new, at least new this time.

"I don't even know the questions," I said slowly to give veracity to the words. "Delinda Paz keeps telling me to ask questions, but it's obvious I don't ask the right ones. Can you tell me the questions, at least?"

"Sure, why not? Here comes the first one. What's the meaning of life?"

I started to say something disparaging, but realized I knew the answer.

"There isn't one. We make our own way."

He stared at me in a way that said I wasn't wrong, but I didn't have it all either.

"I was thinking," I said, this time with a stutter because the idea was having a hard time finding words, "that I was having a hell of a time dying. That's the reason for life, isn't it? To qualify for death because death kicks the shit out of life. Right?"

"What is the meaning of Island City?"

"It's the qualification course. When it floods and you miss the boat you have to do it again."

"Everyone?"

"Some don't think so. Some say there are a limited number of do-overs."

"Not bad. Who am I?"

"Good question."

"I need an answer."

"The other pillar of the community," I said. "You and Birdlegs hold the course together. Alfred Newman and the rest of the trappings are just to keep the players like me moving."

"So, you're saying," he waved over the city again as the rain pelted down harder, "this is all a game."

"It's a construct to keep my interest."

"So it's all about you."

"This version is. The one that has me standing here talking to you. Wozinsky gets a different one and so does Dotty Orland. How much different I don't know."

"What if I'm like you?" the Judge asked, staring intently like the rain wasn't running over his head and into his eyes. "Waiting for a boat of my own?"

"You know too much to be waiting for a boat."

"Really? Because you have a few ideas that feel right you're all of a sudden an expert?"

"Until you convince me otherwise."

A ripple rolled through the heavens and down into the earth. It lifted me. I flew by means I did not understand to a chamber that looked like Frills, only vastly larger. Chairs sat at the front facing an empty audience space. Spotlights in the ceiling sent needles of light to starkly illuminate the performers' chairs. Let the show begin.

The smell of honeysuckle filled the air.

The lights went out and my eyes saw nothing. A voice boomed from the dark. The boom did not hide a woman's familiar voice.

"Who do you bring before us, Penitent?"

The voice belonged to Delinda Paz.

"I bring for your consideration, my queens, a traveler named Daniel Thomas Spader." This voice belonged to the Judge. The setting seemed to prove his point that he was more like me than whatever Delinda turned out to be.

"Ah, Dan T. I know him. Bring him forward."

How I was compelled forward I know no more than how I came to be in this place, but in seconds I sat in a seat in the audience. A light came on and lit me completely. I left no shadows.

"Why are you here, Dan T?" Delinda asked as a light came on over her. She didn't sit with her legs crossed like Max when Max flashed her wares for money. Instead, Delinda sat on a high stool wearing a low-cut white empire-style gown that ran long enough to hide her feet. She sat behind a white desktop that stood on long thin legs.

"To learn how not to fight death," I said.

"How do you fight death?"

"I want to live and I want those around me to live. I think that's wrong."

"What is right?"

"To live and be me, then to accept death not as an end but as a new beginning."

"Why is that right?" Delinda Paz asked.

"Why not? Is that any less likely than this?"

"If you are right, why is death so difficult?"

I heard a new familiar voice as a light came on that illuminated Hildy dressed the same as Delinda. "Hello, Danny."

"Hi, Hildy," I said, and indicated her surroundings. "Better gig than the wheelchair."

She nodded before saying, "Dan T, anyone can be born into life. There are no secrets. Life is the bottom rung. The next few questions are like an oral exam to determine your fate."

"Can I ask some questions?" I asked.

"You may ask two," Hildy said, after a glance at Delinda. "Choose wisely. But first you must answer the question why is death so difficult?"

"Because death is a state of grace." The answer had not been in my head before the words left my mouth. My description of "let life happen" came to mind. I opened my mouth again to see what would come out. "It is the ultimate act of faith."

More surprises and words that recalled past histories. How many times had I faced this inquisition?

"That is not the faith of the living," Hildy said.

"No. The living trust in the words and promises of other living. Death makes no promises, but welcomes the deserving." Still more surprises coming out. They rang the bell of truth. "Death, I've learned, is the black hole with the silver lining."

"Ask your questions," Delinda commanded.

"How many times have I been here?"

It sounded like Delinda sighed but it could have been the wind. A timelessness fell over me. It served as my answer. Delinda and Hildy talked out of my hearing.

"That shall not count as one of your questions because we gave you no answer," Hildy said. "Try again."

"Will I get a boat this time?"

Hildy and Delinda exchanged glances.

"No. The boats are not for you, Dan T."

"Why not?"

"The answer lies in the meaning of death," said Hildy. "Can you explain death?"

"Death is the black doorway to the silver lining."

"And what is the silver lining?"

I opened my mouth but nothing came out. I closed my eyes, and gave it another try.

"Is this about God?"

"Not yet, Danny. Maybe some time."

Before I faded completely away, I recovered. I said, "The silver lining? It's the death of the righteous."

When I opened my eyes I stood near a window. Virgil Wozinsky gripped my elbow. Over his massive shoulder I saw Dotty Orland. She wore a clamshell hat and a cloth coat that looked pre-war. She waved and smiled.

The room had four windows on the same wall. All the windows were open. All had people waiting for boats. The scene called up images of a sinking ship with passengers waiting for seats on lifeboats.

"The next one's ours, Ace!" Virgil said and clapped my back.

I waved at Dotty and placed her between Woozy and me.

"Oh, Dan T," she said.

I blinked and was back in the Frills look alike. Hildy and Delinda still stared at me.

"Do you see now, Dan T?" Delinda asked.

"I believe so," I said. "I am the guide. My own righteousness is not the point."

"Yes, Danny," Hildy whispered.

"Forever?"

"Go to your rest, Dan T," they said in unison.

The light faded and me with it.

Water washed in the window and splashed my face.

"Ace, you okay?" Woozy called.

"Yeah, Woozy, I'm here. Let a lady in first."

"There's only room for two, goddamn it!" Woozy yelled.

"Not my boat, partner," I said offering my hand to Dotty Orland.

"I don't get it!" Woozy cried.

"Not my turn, Woozy. Don't worry. Jesse's waiting for you."

He stared at me in wonder.

"It's because you guys did a selfless thing when you stood over me in the hospital. No one told you to. You just did it."

"What about me, Dan T?" Dotty asked.

"You earned it, too. You shielded me from the devastation portrayed in the photos. You figured out where we were and made a sort of peace with it."

Woozy made to argue, but saw something in my face. Instead he took my head in both his hands and kissed my forehead. He bowed to Dotty and handed her out the window into the waiting boat. His huge frame barely fit through the window and the boat shuddered under his weight but righted itself. I reached out the window and gave the boat a shove.

My vision dimmed and a far-off sound played in my head. Before my sight disappeared I saw a distant silver glow from across the water. The black hole with the silver lining. I'd seen it before.

"Daniel Thomas Spader, Daniel Thomas Spader, come back now. Daniel Thomas Spader."

"Ace, there's another boat!" Woozy called and waved his arm at me.

Dotty waved with one arm and pulled Woozy's down with the other. Her face never lost the smile.

"Come home, Dan T," the voice in my head called. It came in clearly. I wanted to wave out the window at my friends, but the window was gone. I closed my eyes and followed the voice summoning me home.

"Daniel Thomas Spader.   Daniel Thomas Spader.   Daniel Thomas Spader.   Wake up, Daniel Thomas Spader."

The voices called me out of the blackness. I swam from darkness toward light. What I swam in was not water. More like an embryonic fluid. The calling of my name faded as I swam.

Time passed in silence. Perhaps a great deal of time.

I saw light and with it a mist.

I was dead. When I'd been dead before, in the war and other times, I'd seen the light and the mist and knew them for what they were.

I opened my eyes. I awakened on the first day of my life.

The phone rang.

I jumped off the streetcar's foot board and blended with the lunch crowd that packed the sidewalks. It was mostly men in coveralls and dirty skull caps smudged black from the mills and foundries. Me in my rumpled suit stood out. Inside

Giga's, I pushed toward the counter and met Mackie Kincaid's eyes in the mirror behind the bar. He elbowed the man to his right off the stool.

"Welcome back, Ace," he said. "I been saving it."

The counterman poured coffee in my cup.

"Thanks, Jimmy," I said.

Mildred, the barmaid, waved as Kincaid lit a Chesterfield.

"This had better be good," I said to my old partner. "I just got to sleep when the phone rang."

"It'll pay your rent for another day or two," Mackie said, "although why you live in that dump I'll never know. If you had a real job you wouldn't be out all night."

"I've always worked nights."

"Yeah, but now you ain't even working. Join the world. Get a place with a private shitter. Get some chairs, invite people over. Go all out."

"There's nothing wrong with my place."

"The place is a firetrap! It's on the fourth floor, for Christ's sake. What are you going to do in a fire? I thought you were afraid of fire."

"You have to confront your fears."

"Glad to hear it. You'll love this case then."

"I'm tired. I want to go back to sleep."

"Lots of time to sleep when you're dead."

In former days we used to look at life, and sometimes, from a distance, at death, and still further removed from us, at eternity. Today it is from afar we look at life, death is near us, and perhaps nearer still, is eternity.

– JEAN BOUVIER, French Subaltern, February, 1916

THE END

INTRODUCING *LAUGHLAND*

The final offering for this thin volume is the first chapter, also known as a teaser, of the novel *Laughland*. Amos Eliot is one of the most remarkable young heroes in modern fiction as he fights his late father's enemies in the face of long odds and ever-present death.

Laughland is available on *kenbyersauthor.com,* or direct from the author at pdxbyers@gmail.com.

LAUGHLAND

1980: Beverly Hills, California

Ned Greene's goodwill, limited at the best of times, vanished before his first cup of coffee cooled.   Greene's bad morning, spent in the foyer of the Four Season's ballroom, brought him face to face with representatives of those who felt slighted not to be seated with Nathan Ferry on the dais of that evening's International Achievement Awards.

"Did your guy win last year?" he asked each supplicant.

The answer always came back no because those who could say yes were already in the seats of honor.

"How about a Noble prize? No? Then get out of my face! Be glad you're here at all."

A few attempted intimidation, but Greene's massive and well cared for physique discouraged most from that ill-chosen path.   He didn't see why Nathan Ferry's personal security director – him – got stuck with this pissant job, but every year found him still filling the role. He saw it as a test of how bad he wanted to keep his job.   Steady and well-paying employment for ex-mercenaries rarely offered as many rewards and so few risks as this one.

This year's banquet had presented a sterner test of his resolve. To begin with his tux and formal accessories got lost on the private jet's trip from New York to Los Angeles. No matter how loud he screamed no one could explain how it happened "You put it on the plane before it takes off and you unload it when it lands! So where did it go?"

Since Greene's violent temper was well known, the mad race to find replacements had kept his staff in a state of near panic leaving Greene to do more himself. When, with less than an hour to spare, he learned his replacement tux and accessories had arrived he was ready to explode. The bright spot came when it all fit perfectly although he disliked the large size of the shirt studs and the stiff hinges on the cufflinks. His assistant, Norm Brinks, waited while Greene dressed and for at least the hundredth time, demanded an explanation. Brinks still had no answer.

At six o'clock, Greene walked into the ballroom of the Four Seasons, Beverly Hills dressed appropriately. When Nathan Ferry arrived a few minutes later, Greene replaced Brinks with Colin Truax who moved into position two strides behind and to Ferry's right. For the next fifteen minutes he watched impassively, but warily, as Ferry worked the room. Greene wiped the sweat from his eyes and wondered why it was so hot. He waved at Brinks and told him to find out.

"Just did. AC's out," Brinks said. "Hotel says they have people on it."

"How long?"

Brinks shrugged.

When Greene got Ferry's attention he gave him the news.

"Tell them to fix it," Ferry said.

"They're working on it. Might want to relax the dress code."

"No," Ferry said, and turned to another guest.

By dinner all anyone talked about was the heat. After the guests reached their assigned seats, Nathan Ferry took the podium.

"Welcome to the twenty-second annual International Achievement Awards," he said to the five hundred guests. "This year's prizes were hotly contested, and since everyone here has been in the hot seat before I'm sure we can all take the heat for one more night."

He sat down to laughter and applause.

Waiters delivered salads and poured the first wine, a chilled Riesling from the Salinas Valley. It disappeared quickly, and a Chardonnay from a vineyard a little further north intended for the shrimp cocktail filled empty glasses. Unless the courses came faster, the wine would be gone and the guests would either have to drink red with fish or opt for ice water. Anticipating the problem, the staff cranked up the hotel's huge ice makers and raided the machines on each floor of the hotel, but availability lagged far behind demand.

Seated to the left of the head table, sweat ran down Ned Greene's forehead as he nibbled his salad. As he leaned toward his water glass a blow pounded his chest. His first thought was heart attack but then he heard a muffled noise and wondered if the pain or the noise came first. Before the blow he had seen Truax across the table. Now all he saw was ceiling.

"I've been shot," he thought.

This was not the way he imagined he would die. Not in a tux.

Colin Truax saw a small cloud of smoke erupt in the middle of Greene's chest as he heard a sharp pop. He dropped his fork as Greene toppled over backward. He ran around the table and saw a widening red stain in sharp contrast to

Greene's white shirt now held in place by three studs where there had been four.

The stud blew up, Truax thought.

"Napkins!" he yelled. He took the first thrust at him and leaned toward the wound.

The second stud exploded.

Greene's torso jumped from the floor. Tiny projectiles hit Truax, one going in the corner of his left eye. He dropped the napkin and covered his face.

"I'm a doctor," a man cried, as he leaned over Greene.

"Stay back," Truax yelled.

The doctor ignored him and reached for Greene's chest. As he did the stud over the victim's stomach exploded. Both the doctor and Greene screamed. Truax tried to imagine the pain ripping into Greene's abdominal cavity. The doctor rocked back on his heels, his hands tending to a cut on his forehead. Somebody else arrived and pushed past Truax and the doctor. People who had seen the explosions, yelled warnings. Truax stared at the bleeding Greene who used both hands to hold his stomach in place. Truax wondered how a charge could be shaped in something as small as a shirt stud.

The cufflink on Greene's right wrist exploded. The recoil lifted Greene's arm, now minus the hand, and spattered those nearby with blood and tissue. The blast, larger than the first three, tossed Truax backward. He watched, immobilized, as Greene bled out.

Norm Brinks toured the ballroom surveying the aftermath of the dramatic killing. The planning and execution of a man Norm thought to be one of the hardest men in the world to assassinate had been brilliant. Greene's tux disappeared, then came delays in replacing it. When formal wear materialized at the last minute the relief was so great no one questioned the miracle of clothes to fit Greene's six foot four and nearly two hundred and fifty pound body. Norm had helped close the cufflinks.

As paramedics treated Truax's eye, and Greene's draped body still on the floor, Brinks headed for the elevators. Panicked guests from upper floors filled the lobby as rumors spread. He rode alone to eleven and entered Greene's room. He searched the clothes bag and the boxes the replacement formal wear arrived in, sure he would find something. This had been too perfect for the credit to go unclaimed. After he'd looked everywhere else, he pried out the felt liner of the velvet-covered box that held the studs and cufflinks. Beneath the insert he found a card:

BONG SAT

18 NOV 67

He turned it over:

In Memoriam

Gunnery Sgt. Carlos Montoya, USMC

Brinks shuddered. Nightmares of pawing through the bodies of Bong Sat's freshly killed still haunted him. Many of the dead had consisted of nothing more than parts, and all the while a raging Nathan Ferry had waved a gun behind him. He even remembered the Gunnery Sergeant Greene had shot. Maybe he'd shot him, too. The two Marines had come around the corner of that church and both he and Greene had opened fire.

Two questions hammered him. Who waits thirteen years for payback? And, would he be next?

Matt Eliot watched the rush of emergency people as he stood in a corner of the hotel lobby. His hands remained in his pockets where they caressed the actuators that had detonated the shaped charges in the studs and cufflink. Earlier in the day, wearing the coveralls of a repair man, Eliot had placed the explosive device and its timer, that shut down the air conditioner's control panel. The heat in the ballroom room had forced the opening of the doors allowing Eliot to time his attack, and maximized the panic in the already edgy guests. Screaming security details added to the chaos.

Eliot thought of the two disappointing parts of the evening. He had not seen Greene die, but from the doorway he did see the body lying on the floor in a lake of blood with no one within thirty feet. He had taken a risk getting close, but he owed it to Montoya to see his killer dead on the floor.

Second, he would like to see Ferry's face when he saw the card from the cufflinks box. He had no illusions about Ferry feeling a sense of loss with Greene, but planting seeds of fear and vulnerability in that evil son of a bitch would do. Eliot knew efforts to find him would be stepped up, but pictures from surveillance cameras in the lobby would be of no help.

What no one would see coming was his son. Matt stroked the actuators again as he felt his pride in Amos's handiwork. The remaining cufflink and shirt stud would give testimony to the boy's craftsmanship and ingenuity. Eliot smiled imagining the care the forensics people would use in examining the unexploded jewelry. If the truth ever surfaced, no one would believe they were the creation of a thirteen year old.

Matt walked ten blocks to his car, drove south on La Cienega, entered the I-10 Freeway, and drove into the night toward Laughland.

Laughland, and all of Ken's books, are available on line through kenbyersauthor.com. Most are also available as Kindle editions through Amazon.

Thank you.

Proof

Made in the USA
Columbia, SC
07 October 2017